Kno...

Rand...

Christmas in Vegas, but Ethan is still struggling to find his feet as the owner of the casino. He's stuck in the office while Randy's ex Crabtree enjoys Ethan's husband's holiday antics. When it's clear Ethan feels left out in the cold, Crabtree tries to mend fences by suggesting Ethan make Randy's fun and games a main event at the casino instead of a backroom sideshow. This way Ethan can have his cake and eat it too, especially since Randy's the one jumping out of the center.

Randy knows Crabtree's motives are never entirely pure and that the gangster can easily twist Ethan's thinking. Playing naughty elf isn't worth it if it'll cost him his cozy holiday with his husband, and as The Twelve Days of Randy spin slowly out of control, Randy fears his perfect Christmas will come crashing down around him. It's going to take a Christmas miracle to untangle this mess.

Luckily, miracles are Herod's specialty.

This book is a work of fiction. The names, characters, places, and incidents are products of the writer's imagination or have been used fictitiously and are not to be construed as real. Any resemblance to persons, living or dead, actual events, locale, or organizations is entirely coincidental.

Heidi Cullinan, POB 425, Ames, Iowa 50010

Copyright © 2017 by Heidi Cullinan
Print ISBN: 978-1-945116-25-4
Edited by Sasha Knight
Cover by Kanaxa
Proofing by Lillie's Literary Services
Formatting by BB eBooks

All Rights Are Reserved. No part of this book may be used or reproduced in any manner whatsoever without written permission, except in the case of brief quotations embodied in critical articles and reviews.

First publication 2017
www.heidicullinan.com

THE TWELVE DAYS OF RANDY

HEIDI CULLINAN

To Leigh, who loves Randy
as much as Ethan and I do.

ACKNOWLEDGMENTS

Thank you to all the Randy Jansen and Ethan Ellison fans everywhere, and to everyone who loves and supports this series. And of course thank you as always to my patrons, especially Pamela Bartual, Rosie M, Tiffany Miller, Marie, Sarah Plunkett, and Sarah M.

AUTHOR'S NOTE

This novella features characters from the novel *Double Blind*, the second novel and third story in the Special Delivery series. While readers are welcome to enjoy my work in any order they wish, be aware this short story contains elements considered spoilers for the novel which precedes it in its timeline.

Also it's worth noting at the time this story was originally written, only a domestic partnership, not marriage, was an option for Ethan and Randy in Las Vegas.

If you read this short and decide you'd like to try the other books in the series, check out www.heidicullinan.com or look for more details in the back of this book.

CHAPTER ONE

ONE SATURDAY NOVEMBER morning as Randy and Ethan lay spooned sleepily together in bed, their cats curled up at their feet, Ethan asked, "What are we going to do for Christmas?"

Randy had been drifting back into unconsciousness, but at Ethan's question he opened his eyes. He'd have been safe if he'd been behind his husband, but wrapped up tight, his head pillowed on Ethan's arm, his legs tangled and naked, he was exposed. Especially when, at Randy's silence, Ethan lifted his head.

Ethan sighed. "Wait, don't tell me you hate Christmas."

Randy glared at him. "Excuse me?"

"I saw the expression on your face. You were panicking. Guarding against letting me see your reaction too."

Randy pulled a pillow over his head. "I should never have taught you to play poker."

Ethan drew the pillow off again. "I'm serious. It doesn't have to be a big deal, but I'd like to do *something*."

"This is Vegas at Christmas. There will be 'something' everywhere you look."

Ethan frowned. "I hadn't thought casinos would do anything."

Randy regarded him dubiously, then realized Ethan wouldn't know. The two of them had only been together for a year, and last Christmas they'd been in the Caribbean on a private island for their honeymoon: a wedding and Christmas present from Crabtree. "Wait until you see what your casino does for the holiday. I hear last year they had quite the fun decorating your golden demon statue." He glanced at his husband. "Unless you're going to stop them from celebrating, but I advise against that. You saw how much money this season made you last year."

"Of course I'm not going to tell them to stop. I'm delighted to hear Herod's has a history of celebration, and yes, I'll have Sarah put in a call to Caryle right away about upping the ante on the way we put on the dog." Ethan ran a finger down Randy's nose. "I'm not talking about Christmas at the casino, though. I'm talking about celebrating just you and me. The two of us here. I'd like to at least have a tree. Maybe we could have some people over for a small party."

This sobered Randy. "Do not tell me you want to have your parents down."

Ethan raised an eyebrow at him. "You think they would come? They were sure I'd gone to the devil before when I was just entertaining a married man on the occasional weekend. Now that I'm married myself—"

"—domestically partnered," Randy interjected automatically.

"—*married* to a man and running a casino in Sin City, all they'll do is pray for me."

Randy relaxed. He'd met the Ellisons once last summer, when they'd gone to collect the last of Ethan's things from Utah. It hadn't exactly been a pleasant experience. He propped himself up on the pillows and turned to face his partner. "Who do you want to have over, then? People from the casino?"

"Well…I was hoping maybe Sam and Mitch. Crabtree if you think we must, but I wouldn't mind leaving him out."

"Ah." Randy's smile was wry. "You can try to invite the Tedsoe-Kellers, but likely they won't come. Sam has this thing about wanting to be cold at Christmas."

"Oh, that's too bad. I was looking forward to seeing them for the holiday. Maybe we could go to Iowa? But no, they're not in Iowa right now. Where are they? Illinois?"

"Wisconsin." Randy patted Ethan's leg. "Don't worry about it. We'll do something here."

"We can just put up a little tree. I don't mean to make a fuss if it's going to bother you—*Ow.*" Ethan rubbed his leg where Randy had pinched him. "Why did you do that?"

Randy shoved the covers back, untangled himself, and climbed out of bed. "Would you mind starting coffee? I'm going to take a shower."

Ethan called his name, but Randy didn't answer, only double-timed it to the bathroom. He kept an eye on the door as he undressed, half-assuming Ethan would come bursting in and insist on continuing the conversation, but he didn't.

Randy wasn't sure if he was relieved or disappointed.

For a long time, Randy stood under the spray, head bowed, staring at the tile above the hot and cold knobs and the faucet. He wondered if he should tell Ethan the truth. Well, no, he didn't really wonder. He knew he needed to let his husband know he'd read the situation wrong and this had all been a misunderstanding, this idea that Randy didn't care for Christmas, but he didn't want to do that. Not yet.

Maybe it was because Ethan had brought up Sam and Mitch. In the past Randy had spent the holiday with them. Granted, he was often busy trying not to let them know how jealous he was of their relationship, but he'd enjoyed those holidays. They were golden times in his mind.

How was he supposed to explain to Slick he didn't know how to make sure their first Christmas together at home was just as great as those times with his friends, preferably greater?

They hadn't been able to test run things the year before, because they hadn't been home. First there had been the domestic partnership ceremony, which Crabtree and Sam had insisted should be a big deal, but mostly it was rushed and insane. One second Ethan was rolling wedding rings onto the craps table, and before Randy could take a breath, he was lying naked on a white sand beach, his whole body throbbing from fantastic honeymoon sex. And rum. So much fucking rum.

If they'd been home for Christmas last year, they could have gotten over the awkward first-Christmas thing then. Which, maybe—probably—Randy was making too much out of this, and he shouldn't feel pressured about their first Christmas together being so great.

Except all his instincts told him Ethan was going to try, and sure as shooting those attempts would backfire. The problem was they were both working, particularly Ethan, who was still feeling his way around running a casino in general and had the added burden of making a small outfit function in a flagging economy against a sea of giants.

Additionally the two of them *weren't* in that shiny new relationship stage any longer, high on the thrill of being two men in love. They'd always fought with each other, but now their scuffles were over who had scooped the cat litter and whether or not Ethan was eating dinner at the casino too often. They were small, irrelevant arguments in the big picture, but they added up like grit in the gears, and Randy worried how they would whip up a fancy Christmas together in the middle of all the other hectic whatevers.

There was a third liability lingering in the air, and it was in Randy's mind the most important. Crabtree.

Crabtree was, to put it quaintly, Herod's resident gangster, a dinosaur leftover from when the place had been owned and operated by the Chicago Outfit. It wasn't any longer—Ethan had the deed fair and square—but Crabtree liked to stick his nose into everything and make sure things were being "done right" and that Billy Herod, the former owner and his deceased lover, would approve of the decisions Ethan was making. Because Randy had played around a bit with Crabtree in the past, Crabtree also felt he had the right to butt in to Randy and Ethan's marriage and tell them how he thought things were going and what they could do differently.

Crabtree would definitely get in the way of Ethan and Randy having any kind of a cozy Christmas together.

Randy wasn't sure why he cared so much about this, either. He should go with the flow of whatever festival preparations happened at the casino, let Slick put up his baby tree and have his tiny party, and not expect miracles to happen. No question, he was overthinking this and making it more complicated than it needed to be.

Trouble was, though he could acknowledge the truth of that statement, it didn't mean he could stop wishing for something more or worrying that no matter what, this was going to end up being a mess and a headache.

Sighing, Randy shut off the shower, threw back the curtain, and swiped a towel. Once dry, he wrapped the terrycloth around his waist and peered tentatively into the hall, but it was empty, and he could hear Ethan bustling around in the kitchen. By the time he climbed into jeans and a T-shirt and followed the smell of coffee, Ethan was at the table with his laptop open, scrolling through spreadsheets and making notes on his steno pad beside his coffee cup. He glanced up and smiled at Randy, but he made no further comment about Christmas.

It was probably for the best, Randy told himself as he grabbed his own mug out of the cupboard. Still, he found himself leaning against the counter for a long time, trying to decide how to restart the discussion before he eventually gave up and went to gather up the laundry.

ETHAN'S FIRST CLUE that he'd read Randy's opinion of Christmas incorrectly came when Sarah brought him the file of past Christmas party expenditures he'd asked for during a dealer's meeting. She said nothing, only placed the file on his desk, but the file's label was clearly visible, and when they saw it, everyone in the room burst into explosions of excitement.

"The Christmas Eve party! Oh my God, I can't *wait,*" a female blackjack dealer exclaimed. "Especially because Randy's back this year."

"They've been planning since July this time, I heard. It's going to be *big.*"

Ethan's head whipped around at that. "*Who* has been planning?" Why in the world didn't he know about it?

"The staff party committee, obviously."

Ethan had no idea such a committee existed. He felt ridiculous.

"I heard stories of the 2008 party," a male dealer said, his grin tipping sideways and his voice full of innuendo.

"About the cake?" another woman said, looking eager. "God, I wish I could have seen that."

"I heard they had him spread out on the table after he came out of the top, and fifteen different people licked frosting off him."

"Yeah, and that Crabtree took care of the crotch and ass areas personally. In his office. For an hour."

A few people glanced nervously at Ethan,

who as usual went still at the mention of Randy and Crabtree together, but apparently this story was so good even the boss's displeasure couldn't stop the retelling.

Except for a handful of years when he'd been away, it seemed Randy was the star of the casino's private holiday party. There were stories of how he'd appeared in a Santa costume one year and given "treats" to all the partygoers, ranging from kisses to back rubs and in the case of a particularly drunk manager who didn't work at Herod's any longer, a hand job in the bathroom. Another time Randy had been the dealer in a poker tournament where the winner won him as a personal chef and shopping assistant for twenty-four hours. That had been the first year he'd worked at Herod's. Crabtree had won the tournament, and their casual affair had begun during Randy's term of service.

It annoyed Ethan how frequently stories of Randy and sexual escapades always seemed to include Crabtree.

Ethan went home from work that night with his ears still ringing with tales of his husband's Christmas-themed exploits, only to find the star of the stories flipping through the pages of a well-worn red-covered cookbook. At Ethan's entrance, Randy closed it and shoved it casually aside with a smile.

"Hey, baby." Randy's smile faded. "Fuck. What'd I do now?"

Ethan shrugged and headed to the fridge. "Nothing."

He had the door open for all of two seconds before Randy was between him and the appliance. "Spill it, Slick. I'm not in the mood to dance around. Tell me."

This just made it worse, because of course Randy hadn't done anything wrong. Ethan was *not* going to have the I-know-I-don't-have-to-be-jealous-of-Crabtree-but-I-still-am discussion. He sighed and braced his palms against the counter ledge as he stared down at the tile.

"You didn't do anything, and I'm not angry. I just heard some stories about your Christmas party exploits, is all."

Randy murmured under his breath and turned, opening the fridge door at the same time. When he shut it, he had a lime and tonic water in his hand, and he grabbed two tumblers from the cupboard. "They're going to be disappointed, because I already told Sarah I'm not doing any stunts." He slid Ethan's drink toward him and reached for his Jamesons and Baileys from the other side of the liquor cupboard.

Ethan didn't pick up his drink. "Why not?"

"Why not? Because of this reaction you're having right here." When Ethan began to object, Randy waved him silent and spoke over the top of him. "Yes, yes. You're not angry. You look jealous as hell and uneasy for no reason whatsoever."

"I'll get over it." Ethan picked up his gin and tonic but didn't drink it, only stared into it. "I felt ridiculous, hearing them carry on about what a good time you were, and there I was, your fucking husband, with no idea any of it had happened. I didn't even know we had a party committee." He grimaced, then took a generous sip of the drink. "You don't need to abstain on my account, either. Though if there's frosting or hand jobs or sexual services, I claim them all now."

That at least got a smile out of Randy, but

it didn't bleed off much of the tension in his shoulders. Ethan thought he might be about to give one of his speeches about poker or life or how poker was like life, and then his face went completely naked, and Ethan forgot to breathe, because now Randy looked like he might be having one of those rare moments where he told stories about his past.

Instead, he lifted the drink, took a swallow of it that would have burned off the throat of most men, and set it on the counter with a smile.

"Dinner's tuna and noodles, ready in about an hour. I got distracted and didn't get started yet. Why don't you go relax a little bit until it's ready?"

This was the end of the discussion. Ethan went to change and surf the internet, and when he returned to the kitchen, Randy had laid out a spread of tuna and noodles, steamed broccoli, and baking powder biscuits on their small table.

"Delicious," Ethan effused around a mouthful of food. "You could be a chef if you wanted, I swear."

"I thought about it, once upon a time."

Randy tore a biscuit in half and slathered butter into the steaming center. "Crabtree was all set to send me to culinary school and have me study under celebrity chefs working in the city. But I was pretty sure it would make me hate something I loved, so I stuck to prop." He pursed his lips at the kitchen counter behind him. "I wouldn't say no to a better workspace someday. But that's just wishing on a star, really. Wants and needs aren't the same thing."

That might be true, but Ethan couldn't help thinking he was in a position to give Randy what he longed for. He chased a spiral noodle across his plate. "We could move to a house with a better kitchen."

Randy speared a piece of broccoli with his fork and shrugged. "We could, yes. But you're always telling me this is a delicate time for finances. You're not going to risk all that to give me more counter space and a convection oven."

No, Ethan wasn't going to do that. He suppressed a sigh and wiped his mouth with his napkin.

He helped Randy do the dishes as usual,

but he felt restless and frustrated. He couldn't shake the feeling that, for Ethan's sake alone, Randy was saying no to something he normally did and quite possibly wanted to do, and this wasn't going to take them down a good road. While Randy took his evening bath, Ethan ignored his usual night paperwork and paced the bedroom, trying to find the way to bring the topic of Christmas and the party up again.

However, when Randy came into the bedroom wearing only a towel and a sly smile, Ethan faltered, distracted momentarily by the sexy, near-naked, and damp sight of his husband.

He cleared his throat, attempting to regain his ground. "I want to discuss this Christmas party business further."

"I don't." Randy crouched at the box containing their toys, flipped it open, and emerged with a ball gag and a pair of handcuffs. He dangled them from his finger and waggled his eyebrows as he sidled lazily toward Ethan, thumb of his opposite hand catching at the knot of the towel across his groin, dragging it lower. "I want to play."

Ethan did his best to ignore the erotic display Randy made of himself, and the devilish promise the *clink* of those handcuffs whispered in the back of his mind. "This is important."

"And playing with me isn't?" Randy closed the distance between them and ran a finger down the center of Ethan's chest. "Come on, baby. Make me hot and bothered. I can tell you're frustrated by looking at you, and I want to feel it." He ran the cool metal against Ethan's hand, pressing the chain and the rubber of the ball gag into his palm with a wicked smile. "Don't talk me to tears, Slick. *Tease* me."

Ethan hesitated. He had the restraints in his grip, but he also had hold of Randy's fingers, and he squeezed them as he gazed into his husband's eyes. "So what, we're not going to discuss this?"

With a groan, Randy leaned into Ethan and kissed him, lingering with a nip on his bottom lip. "We can talk later. Just fuck me up *now*, please?"

There probably was a man in the world who could resist that plea, but it wasn't Ethan Ellison.

CHAPTER TWO

Ethan caught Randy's chin, digging in enough to make Randy whimper and grip Ethan's shoulders as he drew himself in tighter. Ethan anchored his hand on Randy's hip before teasing his husband's mouth, cheek, jaw, and ear until Randy ground against Ethan and growled under his breath for him to hurry up and get on with it.

Ethan let go of Randy's chin and pinched him through the towel—he would have spanked him, but he knew that's what Randy had been hoping for. "You wanted me to drive, so you'll be patient and accept the pace I establish."

Randy snorted. "I'm sorry, who was it you thought you married again?"

Ethan tugged Randy's hair with the hand clutching the cuffs and gag and sucked hard on Randy's chin. "I could ask the same of you."

Randy's eyes fluttered closed on a wave of pleasure. He said nothing more, but Ethan didn't think for one moment his husband was done acting out.

Ethan made love to Randy's neck at his own pace, running his tongue against the grain of Randy's end-of-day beard, down the cord of his throat, across his collarbone. By that time, Randy was beginning to fidget again, so Ethan decided it was time to break out the handcuffs. He wasn't sure how to implement them, though. What was his main goal for the evening? Immobilize his husband to the bed? Bend him over a bench? Both? What did he want from this scene?

What did Randy want—without having to ask?

Ethan drew back and studied his lover's face, stroking the curves and lines with his fingers. This seduction had begun in the middle of an argument. Unquestionably Randy meant it as a distraction. No doubt he'd thought, *I'll get him to fuck me, and then not only will we not argue about anything, I'll get laid too. The best of it all around.*

Ethan's fingers dug into the underside of Randy's chin. *We'll see about that, Ace.*

Backing away, Ethan released Randy and flicked open the handcuffs, snapping one around Randy's left wrist before leading his husband by the hand across the room to the wall by the closet.

"Raise your hands over your head." Ethan was out of patience, and his voice let that show.

Randy smiled and did as instructed. He made a quiet "*Ooh*" when Ethan attached the handcuff chain over the hook they'd fastened to the wall and clamped the other cuff on Randy's right wrist. "*Kinky.* I love it."

Ethan smiled back, but it was the smile he generally used for distributors at the casino he was about to shred into quiet, tiny pieces for their incompetence. "I hope that state of affairs continues." He leaned over to the dresser and fished out a red handkerchief, then pressed it into Randy's hand. "Since you won't be able to give me your safe word."

He pushed a ball gag into Randy's mouth next, but as he did so, Randy waggled his eyebrows, making it clear he didn't intend to need any safe words.

Ethan couldn't stop a half smile as he returned to the toy box once more.

Ethan selected a few implements and set them aside before he rose and tugged his shirt over his head, leaving himself clad only in a pair of jeans. He glanced back at Randy, who eyed him appreciatively.

Taking the crop in hand, Ethan paced a slow semicircle before his husband. "I'm going to make you squirm." He teased Randy's hip with the tip of the crop. "I'm going to make you beg me through that gag. I'm going to make you shake so much you consider dropping that handkerchief. Except if you do that, you know I won't get you off. So hold tight if you want me to be the one who takes you over the edge."

He'd meant the words to be a threat, to imply if Randy didn't behave, he'd have to get himself off. Except somehow as the sentence hung in the air, all Ethan could think of was how the man who had taught Randy to love this kind of play so much, the one who had years of experience both in the realm of kink and head games, was Crabtree.

There was no way, Ethan realized, Crabtree would let Randy sit out the Christmas celebrations. There was no way Ethan could outmaneuver him. Yes, he'd won a casino from the man, but that had largely been luck.

Randy made a noise through the gag, dragging Ethan's attention back to him. Ethan smiled wanly and ran the crop along his cheek. Randy shrugged, then shivered as Ethan ghosted the leather tip along his collarbone and followed the path with the barest flicks of his tongue. Ethan enjoyed tormenting Randy like this, giving him featherlight touches and kisses across his body, ramping him up until he writhed and moaned. Randy preferred to go hard, to bite and nip and suck until his partner shuddered from the overwhelming force of his attack. More than once Ethan hadn't been able to find a collar high enough and had to go to a meeting with a bruise beneath his ear, a sign of Randy's exuberant affection.

For his part, Ethan enjoyed aggression in its place, but he preferred a slow-burn tactic, especially when assaulting his husband, licks and whispers against skin. Lately they'd added fantasy to their repertoire. He indulged in a little now.

"What if we'd gone to the same school, Randy?" He sucked gently at Randy's neck as he teased his nipple and ran the hand with the crop down his side, resting the tip against his leg. "What if we'd been able to meet each other and make out like this in hallways, in each other's houses after classes ended?"

Randy's eyes opened wide. Ethan could tell he had things to say but couldn't say them. What a wickedly fun game.

"It would have to be present day, of course, in some liberal bastion where we could have been crowned homecoming kings if we'd wanted." He nuzzled his way down Randy's sternum, fingers toying with the knot to his towel. "What if we got in trouble for the way I kept handcuffing you to things? What if someone walked in on you strapped to the supply wall in the locker room, my mouth around your—"

"*Nnngh.*" Randy thrust his hips forward, grinding the towel between them.

Laughing, Ethan flicked his tongue over

Randy's nipple. "We would have been fabulous, wouldn't we? The bad boy who wasn't actually bad, the good boy who wasn't as good as people thought. Only the two of us would have known the truth in the dark places we'd have found together. You'd have loved that part, hiding that secret from everyone. Letting them think what they wanted about us. Knowing they had it all wrong."

Ethan smiled as Randy went limp in his bonds. Ethan was about to settle in for another round of sweet torture, except he noticed his husband's strains were *exceptionally* acute, the noises more than simply whimpers of torment. When he glanced up, it was just in time to see the red handkerchief come floating down, leaving the security of Randy's hand.

Randy had used his safe word.

For a fraction of a second Ethan stared at his husband in stupefaction, and then he scrambled to unfasten the cuffs, fetching the key from the dresser top with shaking hands. Randy had never, not once, used his safe word. Oh, he'd *said* it plenty, but never with any serious meaning. He said it to get people to stop talking about something uncomfortable, to attempt to redirect conversations—in short, he abused it, because he was so cocky he was sure no one would ever make him use it.

Ethan just had.

"I'm sorry." Ethan fitted the key into the lock and set first one cuff free and then the other. "I don't know what I did, but I'm sorr—"

While Ethan freed the second wrist, Randy pulled the ball gag out of his mouth, turning it into an awkward choker. As soon as both his hands were unbound, Randy grabbed Ethan by the waist and kissed him roughly. The kiss shook Ethan, and when it ended as abruptly as it had begun, Ethan was trembling too.

Randy rested their foreheads together. "That's not at all how that story would go."

Ethan, still climbing out of Randy's assault, blinked. "What?"

"Your story. About what it would be like if we'd gone to the same high school. That's not how it would have gone down." Randy ran his hands up and down Ethan's back, nuzzling his nose. "You had it all wrong."

Realization began to dawn—and made Ethan angry. "If you just used your safe word on me so you could *argue*—"

Randy caught Ethan's mouth in another rough kiss, pushing him backward toward the bed, but Ethan didn't fight him—one, because the kiss was liquid sin, and two, there was an edge of desperation in Randy. It lingered as Ethan's husband pulled away to arrange them so they lay facing each other side by side on the bed, Randy clinging to Ethan. Ethan clutched him right back, his hands tightening on Randy's shoulders.

"Randy?" Ethan whispered.

"You have it wrong." Randy pressed his face into Ethan's neck, his grip becoming an unconscious massage. "I would've been the bad boy, yes, but I wouldn't have given a damn what anyone else thought. You could've kissed me in the janitor's closet or in the middle of the football field. I'd have been so glad it was you who wanted me. I'd have given anything in the world to know your fantasy as my reality."

He was serious. Randy's voice was quiet and earnest, and he was curled up against Ethan. He truly had used his safe word for the first time, ever—to clarify *this*.

Oh, my darling Ace.

Ethan kissed him slowly, achingly sweet— it was no longer a tease but a promise. Every toy Ethan had taken from the toy box was forgotten now. He didn't need an implement to wrap this man around his heart. He'd use them all later, to be sure, but tonight…they didn't need anything but each other tonight.

"When you have your next high school reunion, I think you should go," Ethan said. "We'll pull up in a limo and expensive suits and make them eat crow all night long."

"I didn't graduate, remember?"

Ethan drew back and regarded Randy with wide eyes. "You didn't?"

Randy raised an eyebrow at him. "I told you, I got kicked out of my parents' house, and I took off."

"Yes, but I didn't know that was when you were still in high school." Ethan's stomach knotted and hollowed out. "You're telling me you were a minor, and they…"

Randy tried to tease Ethan out of his horror with a smile. "Come on, Slick. It's not even an original story. Happens all the damn time. Then and now."

Not to the man I love. Not to you. Ethan took Randy's face in his hands. "New fantasy. You're in high school, and I'm the student teacher, still in college. A handful of years older than you."

Randy grinned. "Oh, good one. Who flirts with who first?"

"You with me, of course. Bawdy remarks in class, making sure to touch me too much, flustering me since you can tell I'm affected by you too, but I don't want to act on it because I'm trying to be professional." He stroked Randy's arm, teased kisses down his neck. "You talk me into a few indiscretions in the darkened classroom, and once you come to my house, but I'm still reluctant, scared."

He pressed a kiss to the center of Randy's chest. "But the day you're kicked out, you aren't alone. You come to me, and I protect you."

Randy wrapped his arms around Ethan, kissing the top of his head. "I love this fantasy. Except I'm always afraid to wish changes on the past too much. If I'd had too much help then, if I hadn't left Detroit and hit the streets, I wouldn't have met Mitch. I might not have ended up in Vegas. And then I might not have been here waiting to meet you."

Ethan skimmed his hands down Randy's sides, the curves of his body so familiar, so comforting. "I like to think we would have found each other one way or another."

Randy laughed. "Fatalist." He tugged at Ethan's jeans. "Baby, you have too many clothes on."

Ethan shied out of his jeans and underwear, but when he was done, Randy flipped him on his back and hovered over Ethan with a look in his eye that Ethan knew all too well. A look he knew and loved.

Ethan shivered, reaching for Randy as he took Ethan's cock in hand and began to work him. "I thought I was driving the bus tonight."

"You stopped driving the second you started thinking about poor young Randy."

"Sorry—" Ethan gasped and tipped his

head back. Randy had upped the ante by slipping a lubed finger inside Ethan, finding just the right spot with practiced ease, making his husband quake and arch his back.

Randy leaned in and kept stroking and finger-fucking his husband, nuzzling his neck. "Don't you dare be sorry. Not for one second, not for one word of anything you just gave me."

He pressed deeper, drawing a keening cry from Ethan, and they didn't say anything more, not with words. Randy moved his hands over Ethan, inside of him, undoing him.

I was going to give that to you, Ethan thought wistfully, then let go and sailed away to the places only Randy Jansen could take him.

THE STAFF HOLIDAY party planning continued, but after a quiet word from Sarah, the committee no longer assumed Randy would be part of their festivities and arranged for other entertainment, the same as the year before. Caryle, the casino event manager, joined them to make plans for decorations and themed areas of the casino for their guests, and with all these things taken care of, Christmas parties were the last thing on Ethan's mind.

Then one day Crabtree let himself into Ethan's office, ignoring the fact that Ethan was neck-deep in work as he made himself at home on the leather sofa. "Help me think of how we can entice Randy into being the center of the Christmas festivities at Herod's once again."

Ethan put his pen down and gave Crabtree a long, hard look.

Crabtree brushed lint from his suit. "Sarah tells me he isn't participating in the staff party, so initially I assumed you had him in mind for something with the casino itself. Now I find he isn't even working prop any longer. This can't stand. It's not Christmas until Randy's involved."

Ethan did his best to keep his expression blank, not letting on how much he wanted to stick his letter opener into the man's neck. Not that he'd have a shot at actually driving the implement home. Normally Crabtree was a cross between Santa Claus and the actor who played "the most interesting man," but he morphed into a nightmare as soon as he perceived you to be a threat. Ethan had seen it once, when a drunk on the casino floor had pulled a knife and leapt at a female dealer. Crabtree had been sitting fifteen feet away, talking to someone else and smiling, but before anyone else could shout an alarm, Crabtree leapt into action, tackling the drunk, disarming him, dislocating his arm, and ramming his knee into the man's throat. The cold murder in his eye had promised this was the toned-down version of what he could have done to the man. Had this been the Chicago Outfit days of Herod's, the drunk would have enjoyed some time in the back room before the police were called.

Even as it was, Crabtree disappeared before the authorities arrived, and when Ethan was asked who had tackled the offender, he had to say it was a random guest whose name he hadn't caught. The house rule was Crabtree didn't exist, and he was never in the casino.

He was decidedly in front of Ethan now,

however, and it was clear he intended to stay that way. This wasn't a knee to the throat, not yet, but he was going to be a pain in Ethan's side at the very least. As usual, the argument was going to be over Randy.

Ethan returned his gaze to his papers, shuffling them idly. "He told me he didn't want to be a part of it this year."

"That's garbage, and you know it. Your boy loves a stage and a spotlight. You're going to deny him because you get jealous when other people ogle him?"

Ethan traced his pen across a column of numbers, attempting to read them, but all he could see was the red haze of his fury. No, he would never deny Randy anything, and Ethan didn't mind other people looking at him. Not the way Crabtree was thinking.

But yes, he minded like hell that Crabtree would be one of the people eye-fucking Randy, that Crabtree would take the opportunity to remind Ethan under his breath of all the creative ways he had enjoyed his husband before Randy even knew Ethan existed.

"I was thinking," Crabtree went on, his tone annoyingly cheerful, as if he truly were benevolent, not a monster coming in here to uproot everything, "that the obvious answer was to involve you somehow. I'll leave it to the two of you to come up with something suitable. You'll let Sarah know when you've found it, of course."

Sarah, who was Ethan's secretary but had been Crabtree's. *Do you still think you can run my life and that of Randy's because you keep your hand on all the scales?* Ethan lifted his gaze to stare at Crabtree coolly, though his pen began to bow slightly in his grip.

Crabtree smiled. "Excellent. That's settled, then." With a groan, he pushed himself out of the couch. "I look forward to hearing what you come up with. And if you need any ideas, Sarah can provide you with the videos from previous parties."

Ethan had been about to point out he'd agreed to nothing and would do so when hell froze over—and then it dawned on him what Crabtree had just said. "*Videos?*"

Crabtree winked at him. "As I said. Sarah has them all. Give her a buzz, and she'll make sure you have them right away."

Ethan did ask for them, and he got no

work done that entire afternoon, because all he could do was stare at the stack of plain-labeled DVD cases on the corner of his desk. Inside was more than video of Randy and his former party exploits. When Ethan watched them, he would fill in the blanks of those years he had missed, at least in part. He would see some of the Randy he had been unable to know, the man who had existed before Ethan had arrived.

He made it about an hour before he surrendered and went home, got a bottle of beer, and began watching, ready for anything. He hoped for some insight, but he also braced for things he didn't want to see, flirtations and possible make-out sessions with Crabtree and total strangers. He told himself it was all in the past, and whatever it was, he would endure it.

In the end, he admitted he should have known better. Randy Jansen was always going to surprise him.

Oh, his husband was a complete and utter ham in every video, and he was as depraved and debauched as the stories promised. But that wasn't what grabbed Ethan's attention.

He'd been ready to see Randy the man-whore. What he wasn't prepared for was Randy as…well, as Randy.

Randy himself. The Randy who nuzzled into Ethan's hair in the middle of the night and bought him new shirts and ties "because." The Randy who smiled a wry, beautiful smile at him over the top of his laptop when he got too focused on work. *His* Randy was in the videos, handing out presents, winking, laughing, and flirting.

And looking so lonely it broke Ethan's heart every time the camera panned to him.

No one else would have seen it, though with great reluctance Ethan admitted Crabtree probably had noticed too. Randy tried to hide it in his widest smile, in his loudest laugh. It was actually a relief to watch him fight arousal as drunken men and women and an enthusiastic Crabtree licked frosting from his body, because there at least he was simply turned on. The rest of the time, though, as Randy faked Christmas spirit in the middle of everyone else's joy, clowning to hide his pain, Ethan felt hollowed out. This was how Randy had looked when he'd found Ethan on the top of the Stratosphere, when he'd thought Ethan had lost his mind and gone back to Nick. Hurt like a little boy, smiling so nobody would notice.

Ethan couldn't say, later, why he'd turned off the DVD and gone out to the attic above the garage. He hadn't bothered to change his clothes, so there he was in a seven-hundred-dollar suit, sifting through Randy's meticulously labeled Rubbermaid containers, not exactly sure what he was looking for. Eventually he headed to the back of the storage area, where the heat index had to be one hundred and twenty but where there were containers he'd never explored before. There, in the dust-choked corner, he found another piece of the Randy-shaped puzzle.

Six large green and red storage bins stood against the wall, labeled in Randy's neat and angular handwriting: *Christmas*. Inside the bins were Christmas lights, ornaments, decorations, and holiday adornments of all kinds. Two of the bins contained the neatly stacked branches of an impressive-looking artificial tree. One container was sub-headed *for the tree* and another said *room décor* and was comprised of various branches and evergreen wraps strewn with lights, moving angels, and Santas, and a small but unmistakable nativity scene.

The last plastic bin was labeled *Christmas: Miscellaneous*, and that was where Ethan found the cards.

There were piles of them, wrapped in stacks and held together with red and green string, Christmas cards and string both faded with years. There was a list too: a black three-ring binder with yellowed paper bearing typed—as in with a typewriter—names and addresses, mostly for people in the Midwest. Some names had been struck through with a date, and Ethan realized these markings indicated deaths. To Ethan's surprise, most of the cards were religious-themed, and if they weren't, they were ridiculously sentimental in a folksy, homespun way Ethan never associated with Randy. In the back of the binder were folders full of photocopied, mass-produced, year-end letters, also faded, banded together in packs and held together with rubber bands. They told stories of families in Michigan, what they had been up to the past year, what they hoped to do in the months ahead. At the bottom of several of the letters, handwritten notes in shaky hand read, *Thinking of you*, and *Be glad you don't have our snow!* and *Miss you and hope to see you soon.*

Ethan stared at the sea of cards around him, heedless of the heat and dust, lost in the discovery.

"I don't send the cards anymore. Just so you know."

Ethan was so startled he fell back against one of the bins, clutching a packet of cards to his chest as he tried to catch his breath. Randy, who had made his way silently up the ladder, pushed himself into the attic and crawled over to sink against a box across from him. He picked up the binder and flipped through it, smiling sadly.

"I think most of them are dead now." He ran his fingers down the page. "There weren't many people from back there who wanted to talk to the fag who ran away to Vegas, but a couple did. Oddly enough, they were nearly all geriatric. A few were younger, though, and some still send me cards. I should probably keep track and start up again."

Ethan wasn't sure what to say. Every time he had a handle on Randy lately, his husband opened a new door and showed him something that bowled Ethan over. He decided the only way to approach this was with honesty.

"I saw the videos of the parties." When Randy winced, Ethan pressed on. "I'd expected to see a wild man having borderline illegal fun, but instead…" The memory of that aching sadness in his husband's eyes in the videos pierced him anew. "Why didn't you tell me?"

"What, tell you I was being pathetic and trying to hide how miserable I was getting drunk and—" He broke off and sighed, shutting the binder. "The five years before we met weren't my best. First I'd realized Mitch wasn't really coming back, and then he did come back, but he had Sam with him. It was better after that, mind you. But at Christmas…well, it burned my ass a little bit that the old man was with somebody but I was still all alone. Especially on Christmas."

"You *like* Christmas. You love it, in fact. You have all these decorations. You used to send Christmas cards like this, and you saved all the ones from Michigan." Ethan gestured accusingly to the boxes around them. "Why didn't you just tell me you want to have Christmas together too? Why did you look all strange when I brought it up? Or is it that you don't want to with me?" Ethan frowned, shook his head, and plowed ahead before Randy could answer. "No. You *do* want to have a big, sappy Christmas with me. So why aren't you asking for it? Why, when I suggested it, did you pinch me and get all weird?"

Randy tipped his head at Ethan and smiled sheepishly. "Because I'm an idiot?"

Ethan tossed a stack of cards at his husband. "That makes two of us."

Randy caught them with a sideways grin, nodding at the other end of the attic. "Can we get out of here now? Because it's fucking hot as hell up here."

"Sure." Ethan eyed the containers. "Since we're up here, though, why don't we bring some of them down?" He gave Randy a hard look. "Because we're *going* to have a big, sappy Christmas together. Whether you're an idiot about it or not."

Randy's smile was endearing, almost shy.

"Might as well bring them all, since we're already sweaty and dirty. There won't be any saving that suit, Slick."

Ethan would ruin thirty suits to get that soft look on his husband's face. "You'll have to pick me out a new one then."

They maneuvered the bins down the ladder together, swearing and laughing and teasing each other until they had everything down.

"You know I make cookies too, right? Twelve different kinds." Randy wiped a smudge from Ethan's cheek, a devilish twinkle in his eye. "You'll have to tell me what your favorites are."

Ethan took Randy's face in his hands and kissed him languidly, not caring that they were both sweaty and dirty—in fact, he intended to make them sweatier. His heart was full to bursting as he peeled Randy's shirt from his body and shrugged out of his suit coat and vest, aiming them toward the shower.

He was going to have Christmas. A real Christmas, with Randy. He wouldn't be waiting up late, watching holiday movies until

Nick's family was asleep and he could call, and having Christmas with him two weeks early or three weeks late. He would have a tree, and lights, and silly, cheesy decorations.

No, Ethan thought, grinning as he pushed Randy under the spray, neither one of them would be lonely at all this Christmas.

CHAPTER THREE

For a week after discovering Randy's attic Christmas trove, every day of Ethan's life was filled with Randy's Christmas magic.

He loved watching Randy fuss over how he wanted to put things out, worrying over whether or not Ethan would mind his dictates. At first he tried to include Ethan, but eventually he couldn't hold back and unleashed his inner Martha Stewart.

"I want the garland to drape over the doorway, and the nativity looks best on the entertainment center. The angels go on the end table and the Santas on the shelf—I take down the other decorations and put them in storage. The tree goes in the window. That way you can see it from the street. I need to get a new timer, though. And of course half the damn lights don't work."

"Why don't you make me a list," Ethan suggested, "and I can go out and pick up what we're missing on my way home from work tomorrow?" When Randy bit his lip, looking as if he was holding back a floodgate of commentary, Ethan quickly amended himself. "Or, if you're not too tired, we could head out to Walmart right now."

"I prefer Target," Randy said.

"Target it is, then."

Once they got in the car, Randy casually mentioned what he liked best was to shop around at some out-of-the-way places, and he hadn't done so in a long time, which led them to scour parts of Las Vegas Ethan hadn't yet discovered. Soon his car was loaded with lights, timers, and Christmas tins and cookie containers. Now they were in the outdoor display area of a home and garden store, where Randy examined the evergreen wreaths, trying to decide which one he wanted for the front door. Ethan, when confronted with the gigantic blow-up snowmen and Santas and trains and presents, made a confession of his own.

"I always wanted outdoor decorations."

Randy glanced up from the wreaths, surprised. "Well, sure. We have some lights for the outside of the window, but we can get some more. Maybe a lighted garland wreath too? We could wrap it around the prickly pear."

Ethan blushed, but he also gestured to the gaudy decorations. "I meant something more like those."

Now Randy laughed. "Oh yeah? I mean, hell, I'm game, but I never would have thought it of you. I'd have figured you'd call them tacky."

"They are. But they're…" Ethan shoved his hands into his pockets. "I always got so excited about them when I was a kid. I wanted to be one of those yards where it was all lit up, where people would slow down to look." He pushed his hands deeper. "And roll down their windows to see if there was music."

"So did your yard in Provo have plastic deer, spotlights, and piped-out music?"

Ethan shook his head. "I didn't have a yard. I had a condo. I put a small tree on top of a bookshelf, and that was it."

Randy's grin turned wicked. "You have a yard now, Mr. Ellison. What would you like to do with it?"

All Ethan meant to do was get one or two yard decorations, but he should have known better. By the time Randy was done with him, it seemed as if they'd been to every store in the city that sold blow-up decorations, and their final damage report was three light-up deer, an inflatable four-foot-high present with a penguin that popped out joyfully at regular intervals, a plastic Santa in sunglasses riding a Harley with a sidecar teeming with gifts, three spotlights, and a speaker with a long extension cord that Randy swore would attach to his stereo.

"We're going to look ridiculous," Ethan murmured as they stood in line at the checkout of the fifth store, two carts heaped high.

"Absolutely," Randy agreed. He sounded very pleased. "Everyone's going to come to gawk, and I do mean *everyone.* They'll peer through their curtains and say, 'Look at that house, those queers with their yard full of shit. Will you just look at them?'" Randy laughed. "And all the kids will make their parents drive by over and over. God, I can't *wait*."

That was exactly what happened. Between what they'd purchased together and decorations Randy already had, they ended up with a winter wonderland in the front yard. Randy came back from a craft store with a huge roll of white quilt batting and made them some snow. It would be ruined if it ever rained, but it was worth it. It looked amazing. Cheesy, ridiculous, and tacky, but amazing all the same. Everyone did indeed slow down and point.

And smile.

That same week Randy began baking cookies. As promised, he made Ethan confess what his favorite cookies were—spritz, Ethan admitted after some erotic interrogation, the melt-in-your-mouth butter cookies pressed into cute shapes and dyed red and green with food coloring, but he hated to put Randy to the trouble. That comment had earned him an exasperated look and the most drawn-out, torturous blow job Ethan had ever received. He also had a plate of sample spritz waiting for him the next day when he came home from work.

They were adorable, and delicious.

Randy went all out on his cookie making, and he enjoyed every moment of it, but the volume he produced blew Ethan away. Certainly one man could never eat these cookies by himself. There were sugar cookies and peanut butter blossoms and gingerbread, Ethan's requested spritz, some sort of chocolate fudge cookie with a molten center, mint fudge, chocolate chip oatmeal cookies—Ethan thought it would never end.

"What are you going to do with these?" Ethan asked as he reached for his fourth gingerbread man. He was starting to question which cookie was his favorite.

Randy shrugged as he shifted a cookie sheet to a higher shelf in the oven. "Eat them. Give them away. Damned easiest Christmas present. Fifty bucks' worth of baking supplies and half a day's work gives you an almost endless supply." He nodded to the cookbook on the table. "Look this one up for me, will you? Around page two hundred. Fudgy bonbons, upper left. What temperature does it say?"

Ethan spun the cookbook around. It was the red one he'd seen Randy working in the other day, and at close inspection he realized it was a very old church cookbook, the kind Ethan's mother had used when he was a child. Ethan marked the page with his finger and flipped briefly to the cover. *St. Paul's Lutheran Church, Detroit.* Ethan shook his head, smiling, and turned back to the recipe pages, rifling through for the one Randy had asked for. "Three seventy-five," he announced. "Four to six minutes."

"Right," Randy replied with derision. "In this shit oven, it's more like seven. Make sure you keep swapping trays between the racks, and don't turn your back."

It wasn't the first time Randy had complained about the oven, and Ethan wondered if he should make an oven a Christmas present.

Perhaps, he thought, watching his husband swear again at the lack of counter space in his tiny kitchen, he needed more than just an oven. Maybe Ethan *should* look into a different house for them. It didn't have to be something extravagant. Something modest, with a little more room for Randy to cook, for the cats to spread out and play.

When he went into work the next morning, he asked Sarah to look into some real estate options for him.

"Nothing too fancy. A nice neighborhood, a small yard where we can make an enclosed area for the cats to enjoy the outdoors while still being safe. I wouldn't mind a pool, but it's a lot of work, so it's not required. The kitchen is a must, though. It needs to be spacious with a great oven and extensive storage and counter space." He looked around to confirm they were alone. "And please keep this between the two of us. I'm just exploring my options right now, and above all, I don't want Randy to know. I want this to be a surprise, if I manage to find something."

"Of course," Sarah told him. But Ethan should have known. Honestly, he should have seen it coming. Before he closed out the ledger for the day, Crabtree burst into his office, no trace of a Santa Claus smile on his face whatsoever.

"What in the hell do you think you're doing?" he demanded.

Ethan blinked at him, then glanced down at his notebook. "The casino's accounts?" It was a little unusual for the owner to do them, yes, but it was how he'd gotten started, and he did like to oversee things personally.

Crabtree waved this away with his hand. "I mean this nonsense about buying a house. And please skip the part where you bluster about Sarah tattling. She didn't. She asked for my help because it's her job and I'm the one with the connections she needs."

Ethan pursed his lips. "I *meant* for her to look up some listings on the internet."

"Then you should have told her as much. Sarah was *my* secretary, as you well know."

Yes, you never let me forget.

Crabtree glowered at Ethan. "Sarah operates better in the gray than the black and white, so of course she was going to come to me. Thank God she did, though. What were you thinking with the list of requirements you gave her? Did you eat something funny for lunch? Stare at numbers too long? Eat too much raw cookie dough from Jansen's assembly line?"

Ethan glared back. "What's wrong with my house-hunting list?"

"What's wrong, he asks. *Everything*. You might as well put a *for sale* sign on this place while you're at it, to start. It's already bad enough you live in that dive and own Herod's, but I've been able to sell it that you're looking into building your own place and can't quite settle on a builder. Now you want to shack up in a goddamned subdivision like you're some kind of investment broker?"

"I *am* some kind of investment broker," Ethan ground out.

"No. You *were*. Now you own and manage one of the oldest casinos in the city, the one memory left I have of my Billy." Crabtree's lip curled, and he huffed. "And if you think that sort of place is right for Randy, you're a bigger fool than I imagined."

Ethan pushed to his feet. "Listen here—"

Crabtree aimed a finger at him. "No. *You* listen. I've been letting you fumble around like a fool long enough. Do better at claiming both this building and your man, or I'll do what I have to do to protect both."

Cold rage filled Ethan. "What did you just

say?"

"You heard me."

With his threat hanging in the air, Crabtree left the room.

RANDY HADN'T PLAYED prop for Herod's in quite a while. When Ethan had first been learning his place as the new owner and manager, Randy had still worked a few days a week, mostly to make sure Ethan wasn't feeling overwhelmed. After a few months, though, Randy had given up the strategy of working prop to keep tabs on his husband, and the reason he'd done this was entirely because of Crabtree.

Ever since Ethan won Herod's in the infamous high-stakes poker game Crabtree himself set up for that very purpose, the gangster's favorite pastime was getting a rise out of Ethan. At first Randy had chalked it up to some kind of good-natured hazing, but as the months went on, he had to admit something more was at work here. He couldn't really figure out what it was, but it annoyed the crap out of him. Randy couldn't decide what was the best plan going forward either. Should he ignore it and let it play out? Gently help Ethan from the sidelines? Scold Crabtree and tell him to fuck off? Let Ethan find his own feet and defeat his rival on his own?

Randy had no idea.

So far his strategy had been largely to stay out of the matter but to keep a close eye on Ethan and make sure Crabtree wasn't luring him into any trouble. The staff Christmas party had been a landmine he was glad to dodge, and he was proud of himself for seeing it coming long ago. Yes, it had been fun back in the day, and he did have a good time goofing around with everyone, but if his choices were putting on a show for everyone else and snuggling with Ethan, there wasn't any choice at all. It was Ethan every time. He was content to stay away from the casino and Crabtree, keep baking cookies and hanging tinsel, and getting naked for his husband when he came home. As far as Randy was concerned, the Christmas party issue was settled and done.

Then a package showed up on the front porch.

At first he thought it was a package of books he'd ordered for Ethan for part of his present, but the box was too big. When he saw the return address was from one of his favorite kinky outfitters, he grinned and opened it eagerly, assuming it was an early Christmas present from Sam and Mitch. He frowned, though, when he saw it contained nothing but a slightly distasteful leather elf outfit. And he swore under his breath when he saw the note inside, typed on the bottom of the invoice.

> Looking forward to seeing you in this at the Christmas party. C

He was on the phone inside of a minute.

"Randy," Crabtree answered, sounding delighted. "I assume you got my little gift?"

"I'm not coming to the Christmas party, which I thought I'd made abundantly clear," Randy said through gritted teeth. "And even if I were to show up, I absolutely wouldn't come wearing that."

"Oh, but Ethan will look quite silly if he's a Santa without an elf."

Randy shut his eyes. "You're telling me Ethan agreed to play Santa at the party?"

"But of course! He has to be there. He's the owner. What image would he project if he stayed away?"

"And he has to come in a Santa suit?"

"Naturally. He agreed, wisely, that the party needed a little life and theming. In fact, he was the one who suggested the Santa idea. He'll deliver the bonuses to each of the employees. With the help of his elf assistant."

Randy eyed the mesh ass and leather cock pouch of the elf outfit. He had an idea of the kinds of bonuses Crabtree thought the assistant would be giving.

"You're an ass, Crabtree," Randy replied.

"Yours, I'm sure, will look exceptional in your costume. I look forward to a close inspection on Christmas Eve."

Randy swore and hung up on him.

It would have been fine if all that had happened was he'd gotten a stupid costume in the mail, something he could refuse to wear and call it a day, but Randy had his doubts Ethan had agreed to the *exact* terms Crabtree had described, and was equally sure the gangster hadn't lobbed only one bomb. Randy couldn't guess the game, but the odds told him it would fuck up everything.

He got nothing done the rest of that afternoon. After pacing the floor for a good hour, he got on his bike and took a long, fast ride. Even this didn't clear his head, though, and he ended up at the Stratosphere, standing at the rail as he watched sunset take over the Strip. When his phone buzzed in his pocket, he pulled it out, punched back a text, and went back to his silent musing.

Half an hour later, a hand slid around his waist. When a kiss against the back of his neck accompanied the hand, he gave up and leaned into Ethan.

His husband seemed calm, which was good, Randy supposed. That meant Crabtree hadn't done anything else yet, not that Ethan had seen. Maybe there was time to head it off at the pass.

Or maybe this had been his plan all along, to get Randy to tell Ethan and piss him off personally. He sighed and shut his eyes, nestling deeper into his husband's embrace. "We need to get Crabtree a hobby."

Ethan stiffened. "What now?"

Reluctantly, Randy told him about the elf outfit and the phone call, trying to keep things as matter of fact as possible. His heart sank as Ethan pulled away and paced around the nearby area of the balcony, his lips pressed into a thin, angry line.

"He asked me to come to the party, and I said I'd come. When he asked if I'd wear a Santa outfit, I told him I didn't mind. Then he began to sigh and look pathetic, talking about the old days, wishing you would be there, and like an idiot I fell for his trap. He smiled like a sad little boy and said, 'Oh, maybe he could play an elf with you,' and I agreed."

Randy could see the scene clearly in his mind. "He played you. Then called me and sold me the same song and dance, except my version was X-rated."

Ethan threw up his hands. "Why is he so obsessed with this? Why does he insist on making you a sexual spectacle?"

"Probably because he's always enjoyed doing that to me, and he misses it." Randy leaned against the railing, feeling the wind whip around him. "And because he enjoys getting under your skin. Which, I hate to tell you, you make it far too enjoyable for him."

Ethan grimaced. "I *know*. I keep trying not to react, but it *does* bother me. I know you aren't interested in him anymore, but I hate that he has that history with you, with the casino, and that he keeps lording it over me. He makes all this noise about setting you and me up and arranging for me to win Herod's, but it's like he regrets it now. Does he mean to take it away? Take *you* away?"

Randy pushed off the rail. "Okay, first of all, chill, babe. He can't do either one of those things. It took him years to set up that heist to get someone like you in a position to win the casino—which, by the way, you did largely on your own, rolling a ball down the lane he set up. And it's yours now, which means he'd have to con *you*, and I'm not going to let him do that. Which brings us to the next thing you think he's trying to take: me. I'm not a piece of property, I have free will, and I'm happy where I'm at."

"Yes, but I don't think it's you he's trying to manipulate, is it? It's me. He's fucking with *my* head. And it's working. He keeps making me doubt everything. All my decisions, my feelings."

"Then stop letting him." Randy stopped Ethan's pacing, took his hands. "Listen. Everything you've done about Herod's has been to move it forward, not backward. So what if Crabtree and I used to get kinky at parties? Doesn't mean we have to now. I can promise you, I have no interest anymore."

Ethan stared at him, and Randy waited under the scrutiny. "Speaking of parties. Something has been bothering me. You keep saying you don't want to participate, and you reject everyone's efforts to draw you in. Yet when I watched the videos of you from years past, you seemed to enjoy it. I could see you were lonely too, but you weren't present under duress."

Randy hesitated, then decided to offer up the truth. "Well, yeah. It was a fun time."

Ethan deflated. "So you *do* want to do this, but you've been saying no this entire time because of me?"

Randy glanced away with a shrug. "It's not that simple. Sure, the parties were kinky and fun, but I don't want to upset you, and I don't want an evening's cheap entertainment more than I want a cozy Christmas with you. Also, I get that you like to keep things formal with the casino, because it's your work. You won't want to put on a sexual show of any kind for your workplace." He gave his husband a reassuring smile. "It's okay. We just have to find the way to explain this to Crabtree." He took Ethan's hand and nodded toward the door. "Come on. Let's go downstairs and hit the buffet before we head home."

They had too much food for dinner, drank enough at the bar that they went over to the tables and played a bit of poker, then got even more drunk and had to take a taxi home. The timers for their outdoor light display turned on as they approached their street, making Randy's heart rise. *Home.*

Shutting the door behind them, he pulled Ethan hard against his chest, stuck his tongue down his husband's throat, and kissed him as if he hadn't seen him in a year. When they had to break for air, he threaded his fingers through his husband's hair and drew their foreheads together.

"It's you I want." He caressed Ethan's hairline with his thumbs. "Christmas with you. To go to bed with you. Life with you. Please remember that."

Ethan stroked Randy's face, kissed his chin reverently.

Then he gripped Randy's hips, turned him around with delicious force, and pushed him into the wall as he fumbled with the fastening to Randy's jeans.

It was a blunt claiming, Ethan reminding Randy who had married him, a kind of fucked-up reply to Randy's devotional promise. Ethan removed just enough of their clothes to prepare Randy—using spit for lube, one of Randy's favorite kinks, even though he always paid for it later—then took him right there in the living room. It had been a long time since they'd been this raw and rough.

Randy loved it. He shut his eyes and pressed his hands to the wall, doing whatever Ethan said, rolling under the hard edges of his husband, surrendering happily in every way.

Yet as Randy went to bed that night, he could see doubt still shadowed his husband's eyes, and he knew this battle wasn't over. He wondered if he should say something more, reach out in another way.

I'll fix it in the morning, he decided, and drifted off to sleep.

When he woke, however, it was ten and Ethan was already gone. Randy hadn't meant to sleep in that late, but someone had worn him out. He hummed as he lazed about the kitchen, making coffee and poking in the fridge, pondering what to make for breakfast.

When the doorbell rang, he was still in a good mood. He was only wearing underwear, so he grabbed a throw from the back of the couch and wrapped it around himself. He assumed this was a package or a religious nut trying to convert him. If it was the latter, he was dropping the blanket immediately. His underwear was pretty skimpy.

Ethan's secretary stood on the stoop, dressed in her gray suit with her graying hair up in a bun. She smiled at him politely. "Good morning, Randy." She handed him a manila envelope. "Mr. Ellison asked me to deliver this to you right away. He said to call him if you had any questions."

Randy frowned at her, but she only

turned on her sensible mid-heel and headed back down the sidewalk to the waiting car, where a driver was already opening the door for her. He watched her drive away, then went inside to see what this important delivery was all about.

The envelope contained a promotional flyer with Randy's picture in the center, one Ethan had taken of him with his phone outside the Bellagio. The photo was pasted over a closeup of a Christmas tree and ornaments.

Randy read the boldface print below the image.

> THE TWELVE DAYS OF RANDY
> JOIN THE HEROD'S CASINO
> STAFF IN TWELVE DAYS
> OF CELEBRATION
>
> *Beginning December 13th, watch for holiday mischief and mayhem from your favorite Herod's poker player.*
> *Win prizes, get surprises, and be sure to keep your cameras ready.*
> *Because with Randy, you never know*

what will happen.

Randy put the flyer down and picked up his phone. Ethan answered on the first ring.

"Slick, what the hell? Is this a joke?"

"Not at all," Ethan replied coolly, but Randy could hear the hesitation in his voice. "Unless you don't like the idea."

"You didn't want this. You didn't want me involved at all, and I was fine with that, and now you're committing me to *twelve days*?"

"Well, I lay awake a long time last night, thinking. About how you admitted you liked the antics and would do them if it weren't for me. I realized my biggest reservation was that I was jealous—jealous that I hadn't gotten to see any of it. So I decided the answer wasn't to keep you from it but to invite you to do even more than usual." He paused, then added, "Feel free to repeat the cake, by the way."

Randy was quiet for a long moment, processing. "You're serious. You're really serious."

"Yes. Especially about the cake." He cleared his throat. "Do you want to do it?

Because if you don't, I'll cancel the print order for the flyers and tell Crabtree once and for all that it's not going to happen. It's up to you."

So this *was* about Crabtree. "Ethan…" Randy said, unable to say anything else.

"Think about it and get back to me." Ethan hung up.

Randy set his phone on the couch. He stared at the flyer for a long time. Then he picked up the phone and called Sarah Reynolds. He caught her just as her car was returning to the casino.

"Mr. Jansen. How can I help you?"

"Sarah. Hey, can you tell me if Crabtree has been in to see Ethan today? Or did they meet for breakfast or anything like that?"

"Hmm." He heard rustling in the background. "No, they couldn't have, because Crabtree went out of town last night and won't be back until tomorrow."

Good. That was one major worry off his chest at least. This was Ethan's wild hair alone. "Thanks. Another question for you, if you don't mind. I assume you worked a little bit with Ethan on this Twelve Days of Randy thing. Did he seem excited about it to you?" *Or was it more like he was plotting strategy for a siege?*

"He seemed to be enjoying himself quite a bit, I would say. He was quite proud of the idea and was looking forward to it. I think he felt it was making up for all the wild times with you at Herod's he'd missed."

Or more like he's putting a brand on me in front of everyone, especially Crabtree. A warm feeling bloomed inside Randy's chest as he began to understand. "Excellent. Well, it sounds like a great time. I'm looking forward to it."

"As am I, Mr. Jansen."

With a smile, Randy hung up with Sarah, thinking about all the wicked fun he was about to have. After a quick text to Ethan, he hunted down a notepad and a pen. He had some brainstorming to do.

CHAPTER FOUR

The Twelve Days of Randy started out better than Randy could have ever dreamed. For day one, he trick-or-treated his way through the casino, giving out a trick or a treat to each employee he met. It was more fun than he'd predicted. Some people had him do silly things like rub his stomach and pat his head while reciting *The Pledge of Allegiance*, or simply asked to reach into Randy's Grab Bag, which he'd stocked full of goodies and naughties.

The award for best treat request, though, came from the cute new bartender, hands down.

Ethan had hired Lance just three months ago. He was originally from Idaho, ended up in L.A. because a friend convinced him he could get out of Hicksville by making a killing in adult films, then when he realized how tough and demoralizing that industry could be, he backed out and ended up in Vegas. He'd been a customer when Ethan found him, and after an hour's conversation, the young man had secured himself a job. He'd fit in well at the bar, and Ethan was eyeing him for a floor manager position if things kept in the direction they were going.

Ethan also made a lot of eyes at the man in general, Randy couldn't help noticing.

Randy couldn't fault his husband. Lance wasn't hard to look at in the slightest. He was tall, blond, bright-eyed, and full of smiles, though Randy knew from experience if you poured one whiskey too many into him, shadows started to fall around the edges of Lance's sunny disposition, letting you glimpse some of the darker edges of what he'd endured. Like Randy, he'd left home before he finished high school, though he was twenty-three now. If he stopped smiling and you caught him with one of those shadows, he could look as old as Ethan. But most of the time he did smile, and Randy got the sense that so long as the man could keep building himself a new family and sense of center, he would be all right.

The man did love to be flirted with, so when Randy came up to offer him his Randy trick or treat, he didn't hold anything back. He tossed his Santa sack on top of the bar, leaned an elbow onto the rail, and gave Lance a heady wink. "Trick or treat, sugar. What'll you have?"

Lance gave Randy a lingering once-over as he pulled a pint. "What are my options?"

Randy ran a thumb over his lip and lifted an eyebrow. "Well, for *that* menu, I've got to get clearance from the man upstairs. By that I mean my husband, of course. For you though, Lance, I will happily get clearance."

He honestly thought they were still playing a game, but Lance's teasing smile faded as he passed his customer the drink and came closer, leaning over to speak so only Randy could hear him. "Do you think…Ethan could be put on that menu too?"

Randy's stomach fluttered, and with Lance this close, faint tendrils of desire teased him as well. The man was *quite* handsome. He hadn't thought about Playtime with

Bartender before, but he damn well was now. "He could be. I gotta tell you, though, I'm a selfish husband. If I negotiate this, I want to come along too."

Lance gave Randy a *come on* look. "He wouldn't do it if you weren't there, which is part of the reason I respect him so much." He was speaking in hushed tones, but there was no mistaking the rumble of want in his voice. "Obviously I'm not interested in getting in the way of the two of you. He's just so hot."

"Can't say I disagree." Randy tapped his fingers on top of the bar, trying to keep his cool. It was tough. This was a pretty thrilling development, but it had some red flags too. "He's not going to like that you're an employee."

"I know. Trust me, I know. He's so ethical. I love that about him, except for how it's cock-blocking me. I've seen you two take guys away for threesomes before, and I've thought more than once about quitting my job so I could be one of them. You always look like you're having such a good time, and so do the guys who go with you. I've had so many damn fantasies about going to bed with the two of you. I know exactly what I want from you both. It's so unfair, though. I love this job, but I really want a chance to have your husband tell me to suck your dick."

It was a good thing Randy was sitting, because that comment would have made his knees wobbly. "Are you trying to manipulate me into getting your way, young Lance?"

Lance raised his eyebrows innocently. "Why, is it working?"

Randy grunted and adjusted himself. "What if he says no—what if he tells you that you have to choose? What if you can't have both? Which is more important to you?"

Lance sighed. "The job. I'm going to keep thinking about it, though."

He was so earnest and determined, and clumsy in his attempts to be suave. Randy kind of loved the kid all the more for it. "I'll talk to him. That's all I can promise."

"Well, that's more than I honestly ever dreamed of, so thanks for the thrill. I won't be sleeping tonight, for sure."

"Why wait?" Randy pushed out of his seat and stood. "I'll go ask him right now."

Lance began to panic. "*Now?* I'm too

nervous."

"You think you're going to be less nervous with age?" Randy waved at him as he headed out of the bar. "Back in two ticks. Hold that thought."

He left Lance looking whey-faced, holding an empty glass.

Ethan was in his office as Randy had suspected he'd be, checking email. He glanced up when he saw Randy, then smiled and shut the laptop. "Hello there. How's day one going? I heard you've been handing out the goodies. Having fun?"

"All kinds of it." Randy sat on the corner of his desk and nudged Ethan's thigh with his own. "Say. Question for you. Tell me how you feel about that new bartender. As in, how you *feel* about him." He put a lewd emphasis on the word. "For the record, no cop-out answers. I've seen you eyeing his ass."

Ethan threaded his fingers over his chest as he sat back in his chair. "He's handsome, and yes, he has a quality backside. I won't deny that. As for the man himself, I find him to be decent, pleasant to have around, and a valuable addition to our team."

"What would you think about doing more than looking?"

Ethan went still and met Randy's gaze carefully. "I think I don't mix business and pleasure."

Randy sat in the chair nearest Ethan's desk, sprawling into the leather. "Here's the thing, Slick. You're not wrong to have those principles. I think nine times out of ten they're good rules to live by."

"But you think in this instance it's a different situation. Why?"

"I'm not entirely sure, I'll be honest. Something about the way he described how much he wanted this, mostly. I guess what I'm saying is it wouldn't hurt to give him an interview before you reject him."

Ethan pursed his lips. "I can't say I'm impressed that he's prioritizing getting laid over his job. This disappoints me a little. I thought better of him."

"Oh, he made it clear if you made him choose, he'd come down on the side of the job, no contest."

Ethan blinked, then sighed as he settled deeper into his chair. "*Well.* That's something, I suppose. Though I still don't know. He's young, far younger than me, and he looks up to me as a kind of mentor. All reasons that, regardless of anything else, my answer should be no."

Randy grunted. "There's no law that says you can't fuck an employee. It's not smart as a general rule, but like I said, you give him a good grilling before you go anywhere. If you decide to go for it, you set firm boundaries. It could be okay. He's the same damn age as Sam, and you fuck him without qualm. As for mentoring, you own a damn casino, not teach kindergarten."

Ethan said nothing, only ran his long index finger over his upper lip. He had the same interested gaze as Lance did.

Randy went in for the kill, sliding back to his perch at the edge of the desk, placing a hand on Ethan's arm, sliding a thumb beneath his husband's sleeve to seek out his skin. "Let me bring him up to the office after his shift. You can ask him whatever you want. If you decide to bring up this potential arrangement, then that's your call. If you don't, you don't.

Ethan glanced sideways at Randy. "Why are you pushing this so hard?"

"Because we haven't had a new third in a while, and I had a feeling this could be interesting. I have even more of a feeling now that I'm looking at you. I love the way you get when you're bossing another man around. It's great when it's me, but I enjoy being part of the team too. It'd be one thing if Mitch and Sam were around more, but they live too damn far away." He grinned. "Besides. Lance really is hot."

Ethan tapped his finger on his leg. "I'm not saying yes." But Randy could tell by the dark light in Ethan's gaze that he wasn't saying no either.

Randy hummed to himself as he went back to the bar. Lance was still there and still blushing. He fidgeted as Randy approached. "Well?"

"Boss wants to chat with you in his office after your shift." Randy winked.

"Fuck." Lance threaded a hand through his hair and paced back and forth. He glanced at the clock. "Shit, my shift ends in twenty."

Randy couldn't guess if Lance wanted his

shift over sooner or later. He suspected maybe Lance didn't know either. "Go up and talk with him the way you always do. This time I'm coming along. Maybe nothing will happen. Maybe something will. What you don't need to do, though, is freak out. Ethan's not that way, and you know it. The only way he's going to let anything happen is if it's right for everyone, and if it's not, he's going to act as if nobody ever brought it up."

Lance nodded, but he also worried the edge of a bar towel, staring down at the rows of glasses glinting in the light. "It's just…I mean, obviously I really want this. I wasn't kidding when I said I've been fantasizing about this. But I also wasn't lying when I said the job came first. I love my relationship with Mr. Ellison. I wouldn't want to screw that up."

"For what it's worth, I understand the feeling is mutual."

Lance blushed and acted flustered through the rest of his shift, and then Randy led the man upstairs to Ethan's office, herding him toward the elegant set of double doors. Normally Randy let himself in, but tonight he had Lance knock because it seemed a fun part of the game.

"Come in," Ethan called.

Ethan was still behind his desk, fussing with his computer, and he spared the barest of glances as they entered, but Randy knew his husband was well aware of who had knocked—he must have been watching the cameras that told him who was coming up the stairs—and that he was in no way unaffected by the encounter ahead of him.

Lance, Randy doubted, noticed any of this. He was too busy tucking his hands behind his back, rounding his broad shoulders, and playing demure puppy. "Good evening, Mr. Ellison. I hope you've had a good day."

Ethan closed his computer with a smile. "I have, in fact."

Lance eased somewhat. "Did that deal you were worried about last week go through? The arrangement with the catering? I've been thinking about that ever since you told me about it the other day."

"It did. Your suggestion for how to deal with them was helpful as well. I'm convinced it was part of the reason things went so smoothly."

Lance beamed. "Really? Oh, I'm so glad."

"You're an asset to Herod's. I'd like to move you into management as soon as it's suitable, if you're interested."

"I'll do whatever you want me to do, Mr. Ellison." Lance flushed in pride and naked worship. His tongue stole out to wet his bottom lip. "*Whatever* you want, Mr. Ellison."

Ethan's gaze darkened, and the air became charged. Randy held his breath. *Holy shit, go, Slick!* But just when he thought Ethan might downshift into action, he pressed the button on his phone intercom instead.

"Sarah, would you please send up dinner for three from the restaurant?" As she replied with her efficient *Yes, sir*, Ethan kept his finger off the intercom. "Steak, chicken, or pasta, Lance?"

"Um, steak?" Lance said softly, then added, "Please."

"How do you like it prepared?"

"Medium."

Interesting. Randy hadn't ever watched the two of them interact this directly. Lance was all cheeky and sparkles with Randy, but wow, he really was full-on puppy for Ethan, wasn't he? That worried Randy a bit. He could see why his husband was concerned. Maybe this wasn't such a good idea after all.

Though there had been that sexy come-on as well. Damn, this was a hard call. Randy was glad he wasn't the one making it, though he felt bad now that he'd nudged Ethan into the position.

If his husband felt railroaded, he showed no signs. In fact, Ethan appeared quite relaxed as he pressed the button again to confirm their order. "Three New York strip dinners, two medium, one medium rare. Send an assortment of dressings with the salads, on the side. An extra basket of bread, please, and a bottle of that Shiraz we had last month. Oh, and three slices of chocolate cake and a carafe of coffee."

"Right away, Mr. Ellison."

"Thank you," Lance said demurely.

Ethan waved this away and gestured to the couch as he rose. "Sit, please."

Lance claimed one end of the sofa, Ethan the opposite side. Randy plunked down in a wingback chair across from them, settling in for the show. Until the food arrived, Ethan spoke to Lance about the most mundane topics in the world. They talked about the casino, how well Lance was adapting to life in Las Vegas, where he was staying, what he'd done with his friends recently—Ethan put them both at ease, cementing the relationship the two of them had.

It made Randy excited too, because something about the *way* Ethan kept talking made Randy sure this wasn't simply idle chatter, that Ethan was leading Lance somewhere. Randy couldn't wait to find out.

He got his first peek once the food arrived and they began to eat. Ethan had Randy pour the wine, giving everyone a half a glass, and before Lance could so much as pick up his, Ethan spoke.

"Regarding what Randy brought you up here to discuss—I want you to understand there is no need for anything to happen, that everything can continue to go on exactly as it is. If you decide you'd like to play some games with the two of us, this is a separate matter entirely and in no way affects your job or promotion, nor your friendship with me or Randy. At the same time, if you feel a relationship with us has made your position here awkward, I will help you find somewhere else to work. In short, you hold all the chips, Lance, and you alone decide how to spend them."

Lance's hand shook as he picked up his glass and drank deeply. Now Randy knew both why Ethan had waited for the wine to drop this bomb and why Randy had only been allowed to give Lance half a glass.

"I…appreciate that." Lance let out a shaky laugh. "It's like I told Randy. I'm not going to be shy about it—I'm interested in you. Both of you, but especially you. It's just…I hold you in such a high regard, and I value my position here. I wouldn't want to mess anything up between us." His cheeks stained with a blush. "That's not me trying to butter you up either. I honestly mean that."

Ethan regarded Lance carefully over the lip of his glass. "I appreciate that, and I assure you, it's the only reason we're having this conversation. This is new territory for me. Randy and I can find casual bed partners easily. I don't want to jeopardize either our friendship or our working relationship. Despite what I said about helping you find a new position if this doesn't work out, selfishly I would like to keep you around." He sighed. "Though now I suspect I won't be able to get this out of my mind if I refuse the idea out of hand, so I'm on my knees either way."

Lance was beet red now. "I never meant to put you in such a position—"

Ethan held up a hand. "It's fine. Please, dismiss it from your mind for the time being. I don't want you upset."

"Well, I don't want you upset either."

Randy took a slow drink of his wine to hide his smile. This was like watching Ethan with Sam, but it wasn't exactly the same. It was exciting to see something new. Ethan was excellent with a third in their bed—or in the case of Sam and Mitch, four—and Ethan always led the game, but whatever this was with Lance had Ethan at his level best. Probably it was because the stakes were so high, with Lance being an employee. That was the thing with Ethan—he was better with pressure.

They continued to chat through the meal, Ethan lulling Lance back into dull conversation, but Randy could tell Lance had forgotten none of what Ethan had brought up before, that the bartender was hyperfocused on the idea of something happening, that he alone was the one who would decide if something would. Randy wanted to purr, the scene was so delicious.

Then, as they finished their dessert and settled into their coffee, things began to heat up.

"Randy," Ethan said, addressing him for the first time since they'd begun eating dinner, "come join us on the couch."

Randy did as he was instructed, easing himself between the two men as gently as possible. Lance flushed and sat rigid on the edge of the cushion.

Ethan pressed a hand on the man's arm. "It's all right." He stilled and gave Lance a meaningful look. "Nothing is happening yet. I merely wanted Randy involved in the discussion from this point forward. Unless you already know you'd like to leave? Because you can. I'll keep my word, as I promised you.

Nothing will change, neither our friendship nor your employment."

Lance's gaze was heavy-lidded. "No, I want…" He licked his lips. "I don't need to discuss anything. I want it."

"We do need to discuss some things, if that's the case. To start, I need you to state clearly, out loud, that you're aware that what we do right now has nothing to do with your employment or advancement and never will."

"I understand this has nothing to do with my job," Lance repeated.

"Additionally, this is a bit of consensual fun between adults. I am happily partnered with Randy and he with me. Nothing we do tonight nor any night will change that fact. Do you understand?"

Lance nodded vigorously. "I absolutely understand. I would never come between the two of you. Well—I'd like to come between you, but only literally. Not figuratively."

Randy laughed. "God, he'd be fun in bed with Sam."

"Five of us in bed? I doubt we'd survive." Ethan turned his attention back to Lance. "Finally, I need you to assure me you'll alert me if we do something you don't care for. For tonight we'll keep things simple and *no* will suffice, but in the event we continue this in the future, you'll need to select a safe word."

Now Lance looked hungry. "I agree to all of this. I'm ready. Does this mean we're starting? Oh my God. Are we starting?"

Ethan put a hand boldly on Lance's thigh. "We're starting." Lance shut his eyes, but when Ethan withdrew from the couch to sit on a nearby chair, Lance opened them again, bereft.

Ethan crossed his legs and indicated Randy with a nod. "I want you to begin, Lance, by sitting on my husband's lap and giving him a kiss."

Lance straddled Randy with a feral look in his eye. Placing his big hands on Randy's shoulders, he pressed their mouths together.

A thrill raced through Randy as he put his hands on Lance's torso—God, but the guy was broad. Randy hummed as he opened his mouth and trailed the kiss down Lance's chin, licking at the stubble of his end-of-day beard growth. When Lance gasped, Randy laughed darkly and ran his hands up the man's chest, then down again, seeking the hem of his T-shirt.

"Holy shit," Lance whispered, gripping Randy's shoulders. He ground his groin against Randy, whimpering as Randy moved his hands over him.

Randy felt the couch sag beside him. He didn't stop exploring Lance with his hands, but he did lift his head enough to grin at his husband. "You giving me an early Christmas present? I thought for sure you'd want to be the one playing with this fine young man."

"For the moment I'm content to observe." Ethan mapped Lance's biceps, making the man shiver. "Though I'm no Mitch Keller-Tedsoe. That kink won't keep me occupied very long. Especially not with the two of you looking so delicious."

Lance adjusted his hold on Randy, hands sliding to his neck and down his back as he melted closer. "Jesus, this is hot. I haven't done a three-way in so long."

Ethan rubbed his thumb along Lance's bottom lip as Randy worked his hands fully beneath the man's shirt, aiming for a nipple. When Lance moaned, Ethan slipped his thumb inside, then turned Lance's face toward his with a crook of his finger.

"What do you want, sweetheart?" Ethan trailed his wet thumb around Lance's lips, over his chin, down his neck. "What do you want us to do to you tonight?"

Lance's gaze was unfocused, his eyes hooded. "I want you to do me. Both of you. I want you to fuck my mouth and my ass."

Ethan stroked his hair, still studying him intently. "Where?"

"The desk. On your desk. I want you to pound me from behind while Randy fucks my mouth. I want it so hard. I want marks all over my body, I want a swollen mouth, and I want to feel you for the next three days."

Ethan cupped Lance's face as he glanced at Randy. "Get him undressed." Having said this, he rose elegantly from the couch, heading for the door, which he locked with a quiet *snick*.

While Randy divested Lance of his T-shirt and stood him up to strip him out of his jeans, shoes, underwear, and socks, Ethan cleared off his desk. It wasn't exactly cluttered to begin with, so it didn't take long, and the truth was, Ethan had secured the deck for this purpose before. Randy's ass could happily tell the tale. They hadn't fucked anyone else over it yet, so this was a fun new thrill.

Lance looked amazing as he climbed eagerly into position. He was so damn fit, all rippling muscle and broad body, planting his feet wide and prepared to bend over. Before he could, though, Ethan stopped him.

"He said he wanted marks." Ethan put an arm around Lance's waist and pulled his naked body flush against his suit. "Randy, I believe you know what to do."

Oh, Randy did. While Ethan claimed Lance's mouth, kissing him deeply, Randy closed his mouth all over Lance's neck, shoulders, back, chest, arms, hips, and thighs, sucking hard and fast. He lingered too at Lance's nipples, and there he made Lance cry out, gasping into Ethan's mouth.

"This is so good." His voice was barely a whisper, and he couldn't keep his eyes open. "I can't believe this is real."

Ethan stroked his hair, then pressed him gently forward. "Lie on the desk and keep your legs open wide."

Lance obeyed eagerly, gripping the far side of the desk and burying his face in the desktop as he spread his legs as far as he could, tipping his ass up so his hole was exposed, dick tucked, balls hanging. Randy watched, adjusting himself as Ethan deposited the hickeys on Lance's backside himself, seeming to quite enjoy the ones he placed across Lance's ass and thighs. It wasn't long before Lance was begging Ethan to give him more, to touch him, to fuck him.

Ethan lifted his head and nodded at Randy. "Lube, please."

Randy produced the vial, and Ethan drizzled a steady stream over Lance's crack. They both enjoyed the way the man twitched at the cool contact. Far better though was the way he jumped and cried out when Ethan captured some of the slick and pushed his index finger inside.

"Lift yourself up so Randy can stroke you."

Lance raised his hips, and Randy took hold of Lance's cock, which he jacked slowly with a bit of lube as Ethan fingered him. It wasn't long, though, before Lance shook his head and squirmed.

"No, not yet. I don't want to come yet. I want you both to fuck me. I want Randy in my mouth while you're in my ass."

Ethan nodded as he pressed his palm on Lance's ass cheek to pull him wider. "Go on, then, Randy."

Randy moved around to the other side of the desk, and he about lost it as he took in the sight of Lance desperate and gasping, with Ethan behind him in his suit, patiently working him open.

Randy swayed on his feet. "Holy hell but this is the hottest thing I've ever fucking seen."

Lance was so far under now he was floating. "Take a picture, show me." When Randy complied, Lance's nostrils flared, his mouth falling slack. "*Yes.* Oh my God, take more. Take one with your cock in my mouth. With me looking up at you. With him fucking me."

Randy teased his fingers into Lance's hair. "You're a deliciously sexy thing, aren't you? Sure I will, hon."

They took some photos, and then they fucked him. Randy got lost in the way Lance swam in the sensation, falling into a trance the same as Sam, but in a more aggressive, consciously joyful manner. Randy also enjoyed watching Ethan take Lance from behind—his husband was such an elegant top, Randy never got tired of the view—and when it was done, Randy came around the desk and gave Ethan a long, hot kiss.

Ethan returned it, his mouth and his touch promising there would be more between the two of them later, but then he focused on the blissed-out man draped over his desk. "Are you all right, Lance?"

Lance's grin was weary but content, his gaze fixed at something off in the distance. "I feel like that's the first time I've had sex in forever. I mean, I've been getting laid, but I haven't been done like that. Thank you so much."

"It was a pleasure to have you with us." Ethan rested a hand on Lance's hip. "But if you felt that was the first real sex you've had lately, I think you need to reconsider your partners."

"Yeah." Lance's smile faded a little, and he sighed. "I just…suck at finding them, to be honest."

Randy leaned closer. "Say the word and we'll help. Anytime. And I'm not talking about us offering up ourselves." He glanced at Ethan, saw the nod, and added, "Though I'm not saying no to repeating this."

Lance shifted to rest on his elbows, staring up at the two of them earnestly. "That would be so great, seriously. Though I wish I could have given you both blow jobs, and for longer."

"Then I expect to see you in my office tomorrow afternoon before your shift." Ethan took Lance's spent erection in hand, stroking it gently as he stared him down. "On your knees."

Lance shuddered, Ethan raised an eyebrow, and Randy grinned.

And this was only the first day of Randy. *Damn.* Christmas was going to be fucking fantastic.

DAY TWO DIDN'T have any sex in it, not from any of his gift recipients, which was fine by Randy. He had to turn down Lance's offered blow job when he arrived at the casino, because Ethan had been in such a *mood* that morning and done so much to Randy's dick, the idea of anyone else touching it was a hard pass. Randy didn't wonder if that wasn't on purpose—Ethan *did* take Lance's blow job, and Randy played cameraman, then showed the film highlights to an eager Lance afterward. Boy did the guy like being filmed when he knew it wasn't going to be shared.

Randy's Twelve Days of Randy feature that day had nothing to do with sex, but he thought it was pretty fun all the same. He wore a white outfit, carried a rainbow of Sharpie markers, and invited the staff to write holiday wishes all over his body. One of his favorite dealers had done wonders with a menorah that covered his entire ass.

He'd worried a little about what Crabtree would do, but he hadn't been around.

On day three, Randy gave Ethan his cake. Randy stood on the karaoke stage in the bar in a pair of red and green boxers and let the staff and interested casino guests lob cupcakes at him. Within fifteen minutes he was off the stage and lying on a table, and the staff were no longer simply throwing cake at him but smearing it directly onto his skin. Ethan hadn't sent any cake flying, but he did put himself in charge of post-event cleanup. Ethan saw to Randy's left thigh, and Lance took care of his right.

On day four Randy put up a pin-the-cock-on-Randy poster in the break room. Because he was getting kind of tired.

Twelve days was *long*. And a performance every day stopped it from being wicked fun and more like work. This was saying nothing about the pressure to keep topping himself. At the rate he was going, even strapping himself naked to a mattress and putting *fuck me* across his ass was still going to be a letdown.

The real issue that haunted Randy was Crabtree.

He hadn't been around for the white suit and Sharpie, but he *had* appeared for the cupcakes, and he'd made sure he pressed two right on either side of Randy's chest in full view of Ethan, then swiped the frosting in deliberate, repeated strokes. He didn't attempt to pin the paper cock on Randy, but he did critique the paper version and compared it to Randy's own, explaining the ways it was different, and of course he was correct in every way. Again, he made sure to do this where Ethan could hear and become enraged.

Every time there was an opportunity to fuck with Ethan, Crabtree took it. Every time Crabtree did something with Randy, Ethan went quiet and rigid and generally stopped having fun with the game. Which was why on the morning of day five, over breakfast, Randy announced he was calling it off.

Ethan dropped his spoon into his bowl of yogurt and granola, visibly upset. "Why? You seemed to be having so much fun."

"I'm not. I can't keep worrying about how you're going to react to whatever Crabtree does to me."

Ethan grimaced. "I'm trying not to be jealous."

"Yeah, and it's obvious to everyone how much you're trying. Especially Crabtree." He slid Ethan's bowl to the side and reached around their coffee cups to take his husband's hand. "Look, Slick. I meant it when I said I don't mind not doing this. What's important to me is you."

Ethan squeezed Randy's hand in reply and rubbed a thumb against the back of Randy's hand in a familiar, soothing gesture. God, but Randy loved Slick's hands. Long, thin fingers, big palms. He'd know them anywhere, and the slightest touch of them could calm him down in seconds.

When Ethan started to withdraw, Randy captured him and held him there. "I'm not kidding. Let's forget this and go back to our simple Christmas."

Ethan looked at him for a long time, then squeezed Randy's hand again. "Okay." He kissed Randy on the cheek.

Randy shut his eyes and leaned into him. The words swirled in his head a few moments before he let them out. "Love you."

Another kiss. "Love you too."

Randy wished it really could be that simple. Despite what his husband had promised, though, he knew it wouldn't be over, not yet. The shadows were still present in Ethan's gaze. Randy sighed inwardly. That was fine. He'd wait as long as it took for Slick to finish dancing with his demons.

It wasn't like any of them could convince him to go anywhere.

CHAPTER FIVE

THE NEXT DAY Crabtree came to Ethan's office. "You're making a mistake."

Ethan glanced up from his paperwork. "You *don't* want me to have the New Year's Eve tournament in Billy's Room? But it was your idea."

"Not the tournament, obviously. I'm talking about letting Randy cease his pre-party festivities. You're going to regret this."

Ethan rolled his eyes and went back to his laptop. "Honestly, Crabtree. You need a hobby. One that doesn't involve my husband."

Crabtree snorted a laugh. "Very well. Suit yourself." He closed the door on his way out.

Ethan tried to leave it at that. He really did.

Randy came to see him at lunch, which

was a surprise—though to Ethan's chagrin the reason for the visit was to ensure Ethan didn't buckle under Crabtree's needling.

"He hasn't come by to fuck with you, has he? Because if he does, you should ignore him."

"He was by earlier," Ethan admitted, "but I am going to ignore him, yes."

Apparently he wasn't very convincing, since Randy's frown deepened. "He's trying to wind you up. He wants to fuck with your head. If you ignore him, he'll go away. I promise."

Intellectually, Ethan knew this, and he tried to cling to logic and reason, he truly did. But damn Crabtree if he didn't know precisely how to push Ethan's buttons and maneuver him exactly where he wanted him. Despite Randy's visit, Crabtree's seed of doubt wormed its way into Ethan's psyche, and by the three o'clock shift change, he was storming up the stairs to Crabtree's office.

"Tell me why I'll regret letting Randy back out of this of his own free will."

Crabtree gave him a patient smile and continued to idly leaf through the papers in front of him. "Oh, don't mind me. I'm a silly old man who needs a hobby."

Ethan made sure only the hand pressed on the outside wall beyond the doorframe and therefore out of Crabtree's line of sight clenched into a fist. "I apologize for being short with you." He took a deep breath and let it out again. "Please tell me."

Crabtree didn't look up from his papers. "The tension he feels over the party isn't exclusive to the party. If you don't face it now, you'll have to face it another time. And it will only get worse the longer you put it off."

"If you didn't insist on flirting with him so shamelessly," Ethan shot back, "there wouldn't be any problem at all."

Crabtree laughed. "If you honestly believe that, I'm very sorry." He waved Ethan away with an impatient gesture. "I have work to do, as do you."

Ethan lingered in the doorway longer than he should have, but it hardly mattered. Once again, the former gangster had the upper hand, and as usual Ethan didn't know how to keep up, much less regain any semblance of an advantage. He felt especially foolish because not only had he failed to keep the man from bothering him, he'd caved and gone to confront him…and let Crabtree spin him on his hook some more.

Ethan went back to his office, taking the long way to stop off at the balcony above the casino, watching the game tables below.

Herod's was the only casino in Las Vegas where the slot machines were in the back and the table games were prominent both in placement and in play. Their floor workers sought out uncertain tourists and taught them how to play with a soft voice and a smile. They taught poker lessons right on the floor.

They were the only casino shadow-run by a former Chicago Outfit gangster who even the feds thought was dead.

Well, at least Ethan *assumed* they were the only casino kicking it old school. He decided it was best not to think about that too hard or too long. The feds either.

Herod's Poker Room and Casino operated on the idea that the game was the most important experience for their customers. They believed gambling was about advantages and maneuvers, and that of all the table games in the world a man could play, poker was sacrosanct. Herod's believed knowing your opponent was more valuable than a pile full of chips.

Crabtree was an opponent. Crabtree was always Ethan's opponent. He didn't own the casino, but Ethan wasn't fool enough to try to run it without the gangster's advice and protection. The gangster was an ally, but he was also sort of a parent Ethan was always striving to outgrow. As far as the casino was concerned, he knew Crabtree wanted very much to be outgrown.

But when it came to Randy? Ethan didn't know what to think. There was no denying Crabtree had worked to get the two of them together. Did Crabtree still think Ethan was the best choice for Randy, though? Did he think playing matchmaker entitled him to the occasional sampling? Was Ethan hypocritical for denying him? Hadn't he just played that same role with his own bartender?

And while he was musing, why was Ethan willing for anyone to sample Randy *but* Crabtree?

He pushed off the railing and went back to his office. He fired off an email to his secretary. He sent a text to Randy. Then he sent him another.

He paused to make sure he wanted to proceed, then he made one more phone call before he shut off his phone and internet. He locked the door, determined not to let anything short of a fire or robbery take his focus off finishing his review of the November earnings sheet.

RANDY HAD NO idea what was going on, but whatever it was, he didn't like it one fucking bit.

First Ethan texted that he was going to be late, and then he sent another message right after saying, *And don't quit the Twelve Days of Randy*. Randy texted back, and then texted again and again, and then he called, and then he called Ethan's work line directly, which rerouted to Sarah, who explained politely that Ethan had said he didn't want to be disturbed. And that yes, she knew this was Randy. And yes, she remembered that they were married, since she'd been at the wedding.

Randy was furious. Since Ethan had insisted he continue The Twelve Days of Randy, he did, sending out a mass email for his fifth day of a picture of Crabtree playing a very naughty Santa and Randy as his elf. It wasn't the wicked costume Crabtree had ordered for him, but it was just about as bad.

Immediately after he hit send, he regretted it, and in a panic he sent an apology text to Ethan. He also called. Then he swore, got on his bike, and drove himself to the Watering Hole. By the time Slick caught up with him, Randy was so drunk he could barely stand, and he wasn't entirely sure at first he wasn't hallucinating his husband.

He did his best to play it cool. "I texted you." He reached for his glass on the bar, missing it four times before he captured it. "A lot."

Ethan leaned on the bar and motioned to the bartender before murmuring his order. When he finished, he turned back to Randy. "I saw your email."

Randy downed the last of his beer. "Sorry. I was pissed off."

Ethan sighed. "I know. I let him get to me. He told me not to let you quit."

Randy couldn't tell if this explanation didn't make sense because it didn't make sense or because he was drunk. He watched Ethan's hands caressing his glass as he attempted to work it out and got distracted. God, but he wanted to fuck Ethan. Right now.

"It's my fault." Ethan sat back on his stool and leaned against a wooden pillar supporting the faux awning over the bar. He stared off at the sea of liquor bottles twinkling in the soft light above the bar mirror. "I'm jealous. Why am I so jealous?"

Ethan was wearing a suit. His tie was long gone, and his shirt was unbuttoned far enough to reveal a tiny tease of light-brown hair. His feet were propped on the bottom rung of the barstool, his legs sagging open at the knees. Randy wanted to crawl into the vee and wrap the ankles around his waist as he ground their hips together.

Belatedly, he realized Ethan had said something to him and was waiting for a response. "What was that?"

Ethan's mouth broke into a deliciously

crooked smile. "You're too drunk to have this conversation, aren't you?"

Randy took a sip of Ethan's drink. Always a G&T. He set the glass down and put his hand high on his husband's thigh. "I want to fuck you."

Ethan stared at him for a long moment, his eyes going slowly dark. "Right now?"

"Right fucking now."

Ethan ran a hand down the front of Randy's T-shirt, hooking his thumb in the gap at Randy's waistband. The din of the bar, already barely registering on Randy's radar, dropped away completely. Ethan called the bartender over and slipped a hundred dollar bill into his hand.

"I need to borrow your office." Ethan never broke eye contact with Randy and never let go of his waistband either.

The beautiful thing about alcohol, Randy decided as Ethan pressed him to the closed door, was the way it made you fuzzy. It shut off your head, or at least made it so jumbled you couldn't listen to it. You just closed your eyes, opened your mouth, and moaned as your husband made love to your neck and shoved his hand into your jeans. You gasped and sagged and turned around willingly, bracing against the wall and bending forward to open your ass more as your lover ran his tongue down your crack.

The not-so-beautiful thing about alcohol was the way it made you start babbling, saying shit you should damn well not say, especially while you were getting fucked and everything was going so well.

"I don't want Crabtree," Randy breathed as Ethan tongued him deep. "I don't want him like I want you."

There was a distinct stillness in the area of Randy's ass. "But you want him?"

Fuck. *Trap, trap, it's a trap! Don't say anything!* "Well—yeah." *Shit!* "I mean—no. No, I don't. Not at all. I mean—" Randy turned around in Ethan's arms. "I don't want him. Ignore me. I'm drunk."

Ethan looked resigned and stroked Randy's face. "You want him. I know."

"I want a lot of people. But I don't want any of them the way I want you." His hands dug into Ethan's shoulders. "And I will never fuck anyone else again, ever, if that's what you want. You *know* I don't want him like you. You know I would choose you over him every day. That I *do* choose you over him. You could blindfold me and I'd choose you. You *know* this."

Ethan pressed a kiss against the side of Randy's mouth. It smelled like musk, which aroused him, but Ethan didn't seem ready to get back to the good stuff. "I just... I want to best him. I want to *feel* like I'm besting him. I want to *be* better than him."

"Are you kidding? You're so much better than him. You best him every damn day." When this didn't move Ethan, Randy poked him in the ribs. "You think I'd get married to him? Ever? For anything?"

"Domestically partnered."

Randy grabbed Ethan's chin and forced him to look at him. "*Married.*"

Ethan's eyes went soft, and he stroked Randy's face. "You said you wanted to fuck me."

Randy's cock, which had never fully thrown in the towel during all the serious discussion, rose back to full mast with a private *Woohoo!* "Oh yeah?" Randy kissed him and fumbled with Ethan's belt, undoing his pants.

Thank God the owner of the Watering Hole kept lube on the shelf behind his desk. Randy made quick use of it, slicking his husband up before sliding his dick into place, fucking hard into Ethan as he resumed his position at the wall. It was a quick, dirty bone, lewd and raw, Randy swimming in alcohol. He could hear everything going on in the bar beyond the door, and he realized Ethan hadn't locked the door.

"God, I hope someone comes in and sees me fucking you like this," he rasped.

Ethan glanced over his shoulder, breathing against the thrusts. "Maybe you should take a picture. Send it to Lance."

The thought sent a sudden burst of jealousy through Randy, and he locked the door before leaning over Ethan to kiss the back of his neck.

"Changed my mind. This side of you is only for me."

Smiling, Ethan reached back to stroked Randy's hair as he pushed into Randy's thrust.

Randy gripped Ethan's hips, bit his neck, and gave his husband his hundred dollars' worth.

They didn't discuss the Twelve Days of Randy further, and after some private deliberation, Randy let the days continue, though he kept the celebrations subdued. For day six, he gave out cookies. It made him nervous, because usually he only gave cookies to a few of the employees he knew personally, and it was a fuck-lot of work to make that many, but the gesture went over quite well. He decided he'd do that part again next year.

On day seven, he auctioned himself off to play ten hours of poker in someone's stead. He got some grief from a few people about how tame his stunts had become, and Crabtree kept watching him carefully, but Randy ignored them all. The only person Randy paid attention to was Ethan.

He still couldn't read his husband for shit on this hand. He had no idea if Ethan was happy over the way Randy was playing this game or whether he was waiting for something else. On the morning of day eight, he gave up and told him so.

Ethan seemed confused. "What do you mean, you can't read me? Why do you need to read me? We're on the same side."

Randy dropped his box of cereal on the counter and stared at him. "Are you serious? Nobody's on the same side. Everybody in life is always your opponent, Slick. The more someone looks like an ally, the more closely you have to watch them."

Ethan blinked at him. "You honestly believe that, don't you."

"Of course I do. We've gone over this. Everything in life is poker."

Randy had a bad feeling this was about to become a fight, and he tensed, ready to make jokes or downplay things as needed. Ethan didn't argue, though, only sighed and leaned forward to kiss Randy's forehead. "I'm going to the casino. Do you want to come by and pick me up for lunch?"

"I'll do lunch with you, but I'll just stick around and play tables awhile. I'm going to head in with you and get the day's stunt over with."

"Over with. So it's still a chore, is it?"

There was an interesting note of innocence in Ethan's voice, something Randy couldn't read for the life of him. This was what he'd been trying to explain to Slick. Everything in life was poker, and this game he played with Slick was one he always lost, because in addition to never being able to tell what his opponent was thinking, he never had the best of it. You couldn't, when all you wanted was the guy on the other side of the table to win.

Ethan explained nothing, though, only glanced at his watch. "I need to leave. Are you ready to go right now?"

Randy glanced at the dirty dishes in the sink, but the look of quiet mischief in Ethan's eye won out. "Yes."

Ethan smiled, grabbed his keys, and headed for the door to the garage.

All the way to the casino, Randy tried to guess what was going on, but he didn't ask anything out loud. It was clear Ethan wasn't going to tell him.

"What do you have planned for today?" Ethan asked a few blocks from Herod's.

Randy shrugged. "I was going to sing 'Santa Baby' to the demon statue."

"That's good." They'd arrived at the casino, where he pulled up to the valet stand. "Save it for tomorrow, though. I have today's stunt covered."

"What?" Randy asked, but Ethan was already getting out of the car.

Randy followed him into the casino. "What's going on? What—?"

He stopped short when he saw a four-foot-tall and three-foot-wide glitter-encrusted present in front of the head poker table.

Ethan moved to stand beside it, clearly quite pleased with himself. He nodded to the package. "Go ahead. Open it. It's for you."

The casino staff had started gathering around, all of them looking like cats with cream. Whatever was in there, they were in on the joke. Randy eyed Ethan warily.

Ethan motioned again to the package. "Seriously, don't take too long. Open it, Randy."

Randy stepped forward, uncertain and uncomfortable. He glanced up to the balcony and saw Crabtree standing at the rail, but he gave no clues away. There was nothing to do but walk up to the present. He put his hand on the top, pushing the lid up a crack—

It flew off, and Randy drew back. Then he saw what had pushed the lid back, and he froze, too stunned to move. Sam Keller-Tedsoe beamed from inside the box and held out his arms. "Merry Christmas, Randy!"

"Peaches?" Randy whispered, still not able to believe it.

Laughing, Sam climbed out and launched himself at Randy. As Sam kissed his neck and squeezed him tight enough to bruise him, Mitch stepped out from behind an advertisement display, grinning.

"As I said," Ethan said from beside him, putting his hand on Randy's waist, "I have day eight covered."

The reality of it all hit Randy, and he laughed. "You fucking do," he agreed, then picked up Sam and spun him around as the casino staff cheered.

CHAPTER SIX

"I CAN'T BELIEVE you guys came here for Christmas," Randy said for the umpteenth time as they sprawled in Ethan's office. Well, he and Sam were sprawled on the couch. Ethan leaned against his desk, looking proud of himself, and Mitch lounged in the fat leather easy chair on the other side of the coffee table, his fingers laced idly over his stomach.

"Ethan said you guys needed us." Sam had his head in Randy's lap facing Mitch, but now he turned to look up at Randy quizzically. "What's going on, anyway?"

"Fuck if I know. Peaches, you hate warm climates at Christmas. I remember your argument quite vividly."

Sam blushed. "Well, yes. I like snow and cold for the holiday. But family is family."

It was ridiculous how that simple statement went straight into Randy's soul. He couldn't say anything else, so he bent down and kissed Sam's forehead.

Sam stroked the back of Randy's hair, and a prickle of arousal ran through Randy's body. Goddamn, but Slick could *not* have come up with a better Christmas present than this. He looked forward to thanking his husband profusely later.

Ethan sighed. "I called you back here because of Crabtree."

Mitch grunted. "Of course the problem is Crabtree. What did he do now?"

Ethan gave a quick recap of Randy's history at the Christmas parties, of his declining to participate this year, and Crabtree's goading them back into it. "I upped the ante to twelve days," Ethan finished. "Which Randy tells me is too much."

Randy rolled his eyes. "Fuck, it's killing me."

"Good to hear even your debauchery has its limits, Skeet," Mitch drawled.

Randy flipped him off.

Sam frowned. "I don't understand. Why

is Crabtree a problem? If Randy doesn't want to do it, then don't do it."

Ethan's mouth flattened into a frustrated line. "It's complicated." He kept his eyes on the floor, but Randy didn't need to look closely to see he was embarrassed.

Sam shook his head. "But I still don't understand."

Randy opened his mouth to try to explain, but then Mitch said, "Sunshine," with a quiet firmness, and Sam retreated into the couch.

God, but Randy had *missed* them.

He sat up and clapped his hands together once with a broad smile. "Who wants to hit a buffet for brunch? Bellagio? Paris? Main Street?"

They ended up at Rio, which never upset Randy, and two hours later they were slumped in their chairs, fat and happy and ready for naps.

"Can you take the day off work, baby?" Randy ran his hand down the slope of Ethan's suited arm. "Hang out with us at the house?"

Ethan rubbed his nose thoughtfully with his thumb, then nodded. "I'll have to pop in remotely every now and again and keep my cell on me, but yes." He smiled and caught Randy's hand for a quick squeeze.

Randy squeezed back and turned to the others. "How long are you staying?"

Mitch was slumped in his chair with his eyes closed. "Through New Year's. Got a job lined up for the third."

Randy squelched the desire to pump his arm into the air and shout. He turned to Sam. "You got off work that long?"

Sam didn't smile. In fact, he looked distinctly unhappy. "No work right now. I'm going on the road with Mitch."

"What?" Randy frowned. "I thought you had a contract through March."

Sam shook his head. "It was contingent on their fourth-quarter margin. I could have worked through the end of the year, but I'd have had to work Christmas Eve and Day. I settled for a buyout, and now I'm hunting again."

"That nine-month job in Des Moines looks good." Mitch reached over to rub Sam's shoulder reassuringly. "We'll find something, Sunshine."

Sam nodded, but it was clear they were both worried. Mitch had hinted before that jobs for both of them were drying up left and right. Randy hoped to hell Ethan had paid for their flight.

Randy forced a smile. "So. Four days to go. I have tomorrow covered, so that's just three more stunts left. Any ideas, boys?"

Sam brightened. "I'll help. Can I do a stunt with you? Ethan says you have a slutty elf outfit. I could wear it, and you could be Santa."

The image of Sam in the raunchy elf costume made Randy instantly hard, and the thought of him grinding onto Randy's lap while Ethan and Mitch watched made him clear his throat and shift in his seat. "We'll save that for playing at home, Peaches. Anyway, it's supposed to be the Twelve Days of Me. Though the Santa idea isn't bad. I could go around with a naughty-or-nice meter and a paddle."

"Are you paddling the nice or the naughty?" Ethan asked with a wry smile.

"You could paddle the naughty and let the nice paddle you," Mitch suggested. His voice was a little husky, and Randy suspected he was imagining some home scenarios too. *Fuck* but this was going to be a great Christmas.

"That's a good idea," Randy agreed. "I can decide who gets to do what. Excellent. That's done, then. Caryle can get me a costume, I'm sure. And I've already got the paddle. So that's one left, and the party."

"We can sing a song," Sam suggested. "Like Kurt and Blaine in *Glee*. We can even do 'Baby, It's Cold Outside' like they did."

Randy gave him an exasperated look. "Peaches, I don't sing. Plus that song is about a stalker." Then he paused. "But I could lip sync. Maybe Elvis's 'Blue Christmas'? It's a repeat of the demon statue, but I'm okay with it."

"You could do drag." Sam practically bounced on his chair. "We could be Gaga and Beyoncé and do 'Telephone'."

"What the hell does this have to do with Christmas?" Randy demanded.

Sam glowered and folded his arms over his chest. "I want to do *something*."

Randy held up his hands in defense.

"Okay. For the eleventh day, there will be a guest stunt. The show is yours, Sam."

"Really? Oh—I'll do Kylie. 'Let It Snow.' I'll do a dance too, and you can be my partner."

"That's settled then." Randy laughed when Sam launched himself at Randy and enveloped him in a hug.

"Just the actual staff party left." Ethan had the forced casualness of a man trying not to let anyone know how much the thought of said party was making him sweat despite his best efforts. *Goddamn you, Crabtree.*

Randy wasn't giving Crabtree this, and he was done waiting for Ethan to sort things out. They could go back to their weird war after Christmas. Right now the gang was back together, and Randy was making sure every moment was savored. "I think we should do something together for the party."

"The point, as I understand it, was that this was to be whatever *you* wanted." Ethan stood. "But we can discuss this later. Shall we go back to the house?"

"I have to get some shopping done at some point," Sam said. He didn't appear excited about it. Mitch didn't either. Fuck, money *was* a problem. A big one.

"I've got that one covered." Randy rose, trying to beam happiness on to them all. "But don't buy anything for us. Simply having you here is present enough."

It was a sappy and corny thing to say, he knew. The thing was, it was true. Sam and Mitch were here: the sun had come out again. Between this and Ethan, it was going to be the best Christmas ever.

So long as he survived the staff party on Christmas Eve.

THINGS WERE BETTER now that Sam and Mitch had come. But then, they were always better when it was all four of them.

Ethan had long ago given up trying to figure out why that was. He didn't attempt to puzzle out why seeing Randy get turned on by a brush of Sam's hand eased him rather than upset him. All he knew was that when he came out in the morning to make the coffee and found it already brewed, Mitch drinking the first cup at his kitchen table as he perused a newspaper, it was like waking up in a warm and familiar orbit.

Mitch glanced up, and Ethan smiled a greeting at him. "Sleep well?"

Mitch nodded around a sip. "Always do." He set the cup down and kept reading as he spoke. "Surprised you two haven't moved somewhere fancier yet. Not the sort of place casino owners usually live in."

Ethan shrugged as he poured himself a mug and sat across from Mitch. "It seems like a palace after my tiny condo. I still can't get over having a backyard." He grimaced into his mug. "I have looked into getting a different house. I thought about surprising Randy with somewhere new for Christmas. But when I tried, Crabtree found out and made fun of my choices."

Mitch set down his newspaper. "Wish I had some advice for you about Crabtree. Damn gangster drives me crazy. Always has to make you feel like he's one-upping you. Or four-upping you. Doesn't matter if you've done anything to him or not. He's still got to rub your face in something before he'll leave you alone. If he'll even do that."

It was such a relief to have someone finally understand. "That's been the trouble with this whole Twelve Days of Randy business. I can't get Randy to see that dropping the events won't change anything."

"Yep. If it's not this, it'll be something else. The best thing for you to do is find a way to put him in his place with this, once and for all. Though I've never gotten anywhere myself. Don't know how you live every damn day with him over your shoulder."

"I want to win. Just once. Randy says that it doesn't matter, that I don't have to win." He ran an exasperated hand through his hair. "But I *do*. Randy wins by not playing the game. But…well, I guess I want to play." He threw up his hands. "I don't know. Likely I don't stand a chance."

"We got to find something you can win with. Something public. And it has to be something with Randy, because that's what this is about."

"What keeps throwing me off is that Crabtree acts like I need to do this for my own good. I can't tell if it's a trap, or if he really does mean well."

Mitch snorted. "Both, most likely." He tapped his fingers thoughtfully against the newspaper. "You know, I don't think finding a house is a bad idea, though. You have the money. I wouldn't buy anything without Randy's approval, but you can scout some property. And fuck Crabtree and what he thinks of your choices."

"He said I was playing it too safe, that I was aiming too low for a casino owner."

Mitch scratched his cheek. "Well, I don't know about that, but I also don't think there's anything wrong with making a little splash. You two deserve it. Find yourself someplace nice."

Sam came into the room. "Find what place nice?"

They explained the potential new house hunt to Sam, who got very excited at the prospect, and the three of them spent a good hour online poking at real estate. At their encouragement, Ethan considered some more expensive properties—not as grand as Crabtree wanted, but they were fancier than he would have looked at on his own. He was hesitant until he saw some of the kitchens.

They were incredible.

"Randy needs that kitchen," he whispered as they watched a three-sixty video play of a particularly gorgeous property.

Mitch clapped a hand on his shoulder. "Sam and I will scout it out for you, as well as the other ones you starred. The ones that seem worth your time, we'll let you know, and you can do a tour yourself, and then if they pass muster, you can bring Randy."

The plan was a good one, and Ethan was starting to get excited. He smiled at them. "I always miss you guys when you're gone, you know that?"

They smiled back at him. "We've missed you too," Sam said.

THAT NIGHT, RANDY and Ethan officially welcomed Sam and Mitch home.

Randy started it off with dinner. He killed himself to make everyone's favorites in his crowded kitchen, stripping down to his boxers and apron in deference to the air conditioning, which had gone spotty again. The cats hovered at his feet, getting underfoot as he grilled the tuna for fish tacos, and he ran out of counter space *and* table space as he chopped vegetables for salsa and toppings. Mitch came in to pinch-hit and keep his beans from scalding, though of course the bastard tried to eat half of them too.

"I'd kill to be able to eat this out on a nice patio instead of crowded around a shitty coffee table," Randy murmured. When this made the other three give each other meaningful looks, he said, "What, *what*?" but they refused to tell him anything, not even when he started swatting their asses with his tea towel and told them to get the hell out of his kitchen if they were going to be secretive.

He managed a nice place setting despite the setup being stacked against him, and he fed his family until they were full. He made them margaritas and served them homemade sorbet, which his crap freezer had set too hard. This annoyed the shit out of him, but everyone assured him it was wonderful. They also exchanged weird looks with each other again.

If this meant Randy was getting a fridge for Christmas, he would not say no.

Mitch and Ethan did the dishes, even though Randy tried to help, but Sam wouldn't let him, insisting he needed snuggle time instead. He led Randy to the spare bedroom and stripped him back to his boxers, skimmed to his own briefs, and climbed under the covers with him, curling against his chest.

Randy buried his face in Sam's hair with a smile, enveloping him with his legs. "So we're going here first thing tonight, huh?"

Sam tweaked his nose without looking up. "Dummy. Obviously we're going here. It's been forever. If Ethan weren't so worked up over Crabtree, I wouldn't even wait for them."

Randy sighed. "I don't know what to do with that mess, Peaches."

"There's nothing to do." He trailed kisses across Randy's chest, lingering to swirl his tongue around a nipple. "You have to let them sort it out. The more you get involved, the more you rile them both up. It isn't about you."

So much for waiting for the others. Randy shut his eyes as Sam's clever mouth took him to delicious places. "It sure as hell seems like it's about me."

"You're the object of the conversation, but you're not really the subject." Sam paused to suck on Randy again, eventually coming off his areola with an audible *pop* that sent gooseflesh across Randy's arms. "They're talking to each other about power. Best you stay out of it."

Randy threaded his fingers into Sam's hair, guiding him toward his sternum and then pushing him meaningfully downward. "I'm going to need something to distract me, then."

"*Mmm.*" Sam smiled against Randy's abdomen before kissing it openmouthed. "I'll have to see what I can do about that."

When Mitch and Ethan came into the room, Sam had Randy's cock out and halfway into his mouth, his lips just brushing the tip. Randy grabbed for his hair to push him all the way on, but it was too late. Mitch reached him first.

"Oh, I see. Some people thought they could get started without us." Mitch pulled a whimpering Sam to him, leaving Randy's cock bobbing lonely against the air. "Ethan, what do you think we should do about that?"

Ethan remained in the doorway, coolly watching the scene, but he had a ghost of a smile on his face. He also still wore his suit, though he'd removed the jacket and now stood only in his shirt, tie, vest, and trousers. "I think, just this once, I'm willing to overlook it." He pushed off the door and approached Sam, stroking his face with a tender gesture. "I think we've all been impatient for our reunion."

Sam made a soft noise in his throat and regarded Ethan with puppy-dog eyes, but Randy wasn't playing. "Then the two of you need to fucking get naked and start telling us whose cocks to suck, because I am so past ready to get laid it's not funny."

For once, nobody argued or teased—everyone really was that eager for it, because the next thing Randy knew, all four of them were stripped bare, he was draped in Ethan's arms, and Sam was back to giving him a blow job while Mitch fingered him. It was a damn pretty sight, Sam with his ass in the air getting opened up while he sucked cock, and of course Sam was nothing but helpless sighs and moans until the rest of them were as under him as he was them. Randy was wired and ready to fuck right then and there, but Ethan slowed them down.

"Randy, on your back, pillow under your ass. Sam, you lie on top of him." Ethan murmured something to Mitch they couldn't hear, as first Randy and then Sam went into position.

Whatever he said, Mitch nodded and grunted with approval. "I like it." He watched Randy and Sam as they twined lewdly against one another, seemed to consider something, and leaned forward to speak softly in Sam's ear.

"You have my permission."

Randy's heart skipped a beat, and Sam's pupils dilated before he turned to press a kiss on his husband's cheek. They'd just been granted permission to kiss each other if they wanted, a rare allowance. Randy wasn't going to let it slip by.

Before he could think any further on that, though, Randy felt cool fingers at his hole, and at the same moment Sam gasped and shuddered over top of him.

Mitch settled in beside them, lying on his side several feet away—Ethan and Randy had upgraded the spare bedroom to a king-size bed for just this purpose. "I do love watching you eat out my husband's ass, Ellison. Though spank him a bit for me, please. He'll perform a lot better if you make his skin more sensitive."

Ethan rose, his face coming into view over the moon of Sam's ass. He wiped his lips delicately with his long fingers. "Good idea. Sam, brace yourself on your elbows and look into Randy's face while I swat you. Let him see how much you like me spanking you."

Whimpering, Sam complied. Randy's heart skipped a beat as Sam gazed at him, lost in a sensual haze, shamed and brazen.

God, but Sam was so pretty when he was spanked. Randy hadn't ever been this close to his face, watching his expressions change. His cheeks stained with blush, his mouth fell open, his eyes became unfocused, yet they never left Randy's, just as he'd been ordered. He gasped, he grunted, he bit his lip, but he remained in place, except for the thrusting forward of his body as Ethan's palms slapped across his flesh.

"Tell Randy where Ethan's spanking you, Sunshine." Mitch's voice was low and gruff. "On your lovely cheeks, yes, but where else?"

Sam's cheeks went bright red with shame, but he didn't look away from Randy. "My hole. Right on my hole."

Randy's eyebrows shot up as he glanced over Sam's shoulder. Heard the force of the *smacks* Ethan rained down, realized where they were landing. "And you're sticking your ass up and taking it?"

Sam nodded, his blush deepening. He quaked not with pain but with shame. "Mitch has been training me."

Mitch leaned over and pinched Sam's ass, making him jump. "Tell him, Sam. Tell Ethan what you want. What I want to hear you say."

Sam looked ready to die of embarrassment, but still he didn't shut his eyes. "Please, Ethan." He spread his legs wider. "Spank my hole harder."

With a hardening of his expression that made Randy shiver, Ethan did as Sam bade him to, and now Sam *did* squeal, no longer able to keep his eyes open, barely able to stop himself from collapsing onto Randy. Randy helped him out by holding him up, until he couldn't stand it any longer and drew Sam's head onto his shoulder so he could reach around and tug at his nipples.

"Fuck, you're hot, honey. How much longer you going to have him wail on you?"

Mitch answered for his husband, still observing the show in that sexy, detached way he had. "Give him a little longer. Really push him to the edge. You want to go until he's almost crying, then pull him open and eat him out. Randy won't need any other Christmas present after that."

"Please," Sam begged, burrowing his face into Randy's shoulder. "*Oh, God.*"

Mitch shook his head, looking like he really wanted a cigarette. "Nope. Not ready yet. Twist him a little there, Jansen. Let me hear some good whines."

Sam gave them some whines, all right, and some pleas, and some incoherent babble. Then there came a moment when everything shifted, the sweet torture melting away a bit too much toward simple torture, and before Mitch could even say something, Ethan stopped, dropping to his knees. Pulling Sam's cheeks open wide with several fingers on each side, he gave Randy a look that had him shivering. Finally, Ethan lowered his mouth.

Sam came unhinged.

He didn't scream, but he let out a kind of guttural sound that made Randy startle and want to ask if Sam was all right. He never so much as got a word out, though, because before he got a chance, his mouth was full of Sam. Lips, teeth, tongue—Sam only stopped once to fumble for Randy's hand, reapply it to his nipple, and coax his fingers into rough tugs and twists. All the while, down below, Sam's cock ground against his own.

Randy gave over to all of it. To Sam's kisses, to the pressure of his groin, to Ethan's fingers at his own ass, urging him open. He slid under Sam, Ethan, all of them, until everything was a haze of sensation, an endless orgy of pleasure.

At some point things shifted again, and after one last kiss from Sam, it was Ethan's mouth on his, Ethan pushing deep inside him. He was aware, dimly, of Mitch fucking Sam hard into the mattress beside him, but he let that knowledge drift away. As much as he was glad the Keller-Tedsoes had returned to his life, in this exact moment, there was only one man that existed in the universe.

I love you, he tried to say, but he was so fucked out he could only gaze up at Ethan from pink mist as his husband pounded him.

Except Ethan must have heard him somehow, because he paused, stroked his face, and smiled at him before going back to blowing his brains out via his dick.

ETHAN AND MITCH sat up at the kitchen table, enjoying postcoital beers as their husbands slept the fucked-out sleep of the just. Mitch gave Ethan the report he'd been waiting all day for, which was that he and Sam had found three promising properties for him, and Ethan made room in his schedule the next day to view two of them himself.

At one in the morning, Ethan roused Randy and lured him back to their bed. Ethan had intended to sleep, he truly had, but he couldn't help lying awake, thinking about his next day's plans.

He was also, despite his best efforts, thinking too much about besting Crabtree.

To truly win, he needed something more definitive. Something public. Ethan could see the shape of it in his head, of what it would have to be like. But he couldn't translate it into anything else.

"Quit worrying about it."

Ethan turned in bed and gazed at his husband in the darkness. "I didn't think you were awake."

"I wasn't, but then I tried to snuggle up to you and found you were sitting up, and I knew you were worrying about Crabtree." Randy sat up too, leaning on Ethan's shoulder.

Ethan kissed him gently on the lips, brushing against him a second time when the contact made Randy go soft. "Sorry, Ace."

"Crabtree has seen the way I melt for you," Randy whispered. "Everybody has. The only reason he gets to you is you're the only one who doesn't know you've already won."

Ethan licked the bottom of Randy's chin, sucked on the line of his jaw, pausing when Randy cried out.

Randy stroked his neck, nuzzled his chin. "Please don't stop."

Though Ethan was surprised, the emotion faded quickly under desire as he resumed trailing kisses toward his husband's ear. "I thought you might be too worn out."

"I am, a little…but those guys got me too hot and bothered." He palmed Ethan's growing erection. "Plus I know you have more for me, baby. And I'm a greedy fucker. I want it all for myself."

Heat and a sense of power built inside him, and he pushed Randy down onto the bed. All he knew was the sounds Randy made when he kissed his stomach, the tension in his arched back as Ethan licked his way up Randy's sternum. *This.* This was what he needed. He opened his mouth, shifted to the left, and came down over Randy's nipple.

Randy fisted his hands into Ethan's hair and cried out. Randy surrendered to more than just pleasure: he surrendered to safety, to Ethan. Ethan realized this was his edge over Crabtree, this aspect of Randy was his and his alone. This Randy had nothing to do with stunts or leers. He was gentle and vulnerable, the core self of Randy all those stunts and leers sheltered.

It wasn't who controlled Randy. It was who Randy surrendered to. Not sexually. Not socially. This. Sweet, soft Randy who didn't want a raunchy elf costume or a hot foursome. He wanted family. He wanted a safe place to bake cookies and someone to look at the lights with him.

Like a bud blossoming in the darkness, Ethan knew how to best Crabtree.

The thought never left him, not while he made love to Randy, not as he brought the others in and made a sex-sated nest in their bed. In the days that followed, as Randy finished the last of his stunts leading up to the party, Ethan kept imagining his moment coming at last, and he couldn't wait for it to happen. When they were all sitting at the bar and Crabtree came up looking smug and satisfied, Ethan was ready.

"What will you be doing for the party, Randy?" Crabtree asked. His hand slid down Randy's back, a subtle but meaningful caress.

Ethan said nothing, only watched Randy war between liking the touch and moving away from it. For the first time since he'd taken ownership of the casino, however, the gangster's needling didn't get to him in the slightest.

Mitch ignored Crabtree, reaching for a cigarette. Randy remained stony-faced.

"You can't back out of it," Crabtree warned. "Everyone's eager for the twelfth day. Will you follow through?"

"I'll do it," Randy snapped, and this time he did pull away.

Ethan held his breath for a moment, then let it out and cleared his throat. "If Randy is willing, I have an idea."

Crabtree raised an eyebrow. "Oh?"

Randy seemed surprised but pleased. "Let's hear it, Slick."

"I think," Ethan said, keeping his voice cool and detached, "Randy should let everyone in the casino who wants to give him a kiss. One kiss. Wherever they'd like to kiss him."

No one said anything. Mitch looked apoplectic: he viewed kisses as the one line not to be crossed. He'd let an entire football team fuck Sam if his husband was game for it, but even Ethan and Randy had to have permission to kiss Sam anywhere near his mouth, during sex or not. Sam didn't appear to be quite as scandalized, but he was close.

Randy seemed slightly wary, as if he didn't mind but was sure somehow this would go wrong. Ethan was confident this was the perfect plan, though. He was sure if he and Crabtree both kissed Randy, the difference between them would be obvious. That tenderness would come through, and Ethan would be the obvious winner.

Crabtree was poker-blank. "I think that's a fine idea. I think he should do it blindfolded."

Ethan went still.

You could blindfold me and I'd choose you.

Randy had said that to him but days ago, in the privacy of the Watering Hole's office, right before he'd fucked Ethan. Had Crabtree found out somehow? Was that simply a lucky guess? God*damn* it, but how the hell did the man always know exactly what to say?

It was a trap. It was a fucking trap. Now the game wasn't simply who was the better kisser. Now the game was would Randy know the difference between the two of them in addition to who would be the better kisser. The odds were different for this game, the stakes much higher. This wasn't the setup Ethan had anticipated at all.

Yet his only choice was to accept it.

He could see Randy about to say no. Ethan smothered his panic and doubt and dredged up the smile he reserved for such moments with Crabtree.

You're the only one who doesn't see that you've already won.

It was time to see for himself, then.

"Sounds good to me." Ethan turned to Randy. "What do you think? Are you willing?"

Randy didn't look at Crabtree, too busy studying Ethan as if he were a safe he was trying to crack. "I'll do whatever you want, Slick." *And not do whatever you don't want*, his gaze promised just as clearly.

Ethan inclined his head at Crabtree. "Then it's settled."

The gauntlet was thrown. Now all Ethan had to do was not get punched into the ground with it.

CHAPTER SEVEN

IT TOOK EVERY ounce of Ethan's control not to try to rig the kissing stunt.

In his mind he was even calling it "the contest," because really, at this point, that's what it was. Obviously Crabtree was in on the extra layer, as were Mitch and Sam. Some staff seemed to sense a tremor in the Force as they helped decorate for the party that evening, but he couldn't be entirely sure.

The only one who absolutely didn't see it as a battle was Randy.

Oh, he knew something was up, and there was no question in Ethan's mind that his husband was angry. He started out concerned. He spent the morning trying to argue his way out of the party.

"We don't need to do this." Randy leaned into Ethan with his hand braced against the counter. "Let's just go. Skip town. We can go up to the mountains, all four of us, and spend a beautiful Christmas full of snow and cold and no casino."

"We were going to have Christmas here," Ethan pointed out. "Our first."

"We can take everything. Decorations, presents—hell, I can have us a full-course meal packed and ready by three." He let go of the counter and gripped Ethan's arm. "Come on, Slick. Don't do this. All it's going to do is cause trouble."

"No." Ethan shook his head. "I want this settled."

Randy turned away from Ethan and started slamming dishes around in the pretense of making himself breakfast. "It's already settled, damn it." He waved a coffee mug at Ethan's face. "What the hell do I have to do to prove to you that I love you and not him?"

"It's not that," Ethan said, trying to gentle him. "It isn't even about you, really."

"Then why the fuck do I have to be your goddamned puppet?" Randy slammed the mug down so hard on the counter that Ethan expected to see it crack in half. It held together, though, even when Randy swore and swept it into the sink with a clatter.

Randy tried to leave, but Ethan stopped him with a touch on his wrist.

"Please." Ethan threaded his fingers into Randy's, his stomach flipping over in his gut. The crack of that mug kept ringing in his ears. "If you truly want me to call it off, I will. Let me tell you why I want to do this first, though, *please.*"

Randy snorted. "I know exactly why you want to do this."

"Do you? Because I don't understand how you can tell me life is a poker game and everyone is your opponent and then insist I leave this alone. I *know* you'll choose me over him, but he doesn't seem to get that, and it's making me insane. I want to make him see." Ethan let go of Randy and ran a hand through his hair in exasperation. "You're right, though, I'm making you a puppet, and that's disgusting. I'll call it off—"

Randy stopped him with a kiss, lingering against his lips. "No. We're going to do it. I still know how this is going to go down, but we're going to do it—with the caveat that afterward you're going to listen to me while I explain some things. I've been waiting for you to figure them out on your own, but this is a bit too much, I think. So we'll do this one last time, and then I'm giving you some truth. Okay?"

Ethan didn't like the sound of this, but it wasn't as if he could argue. "All right."

He'd risen that morning fired up and ready to take on Crabtree, but now Randy had him doubting himself. He did his best to rally during the day, but when Mitch came to his office at five o'clock, Ethan sat back in his chair and let some of his mask fall.

Mitch settled in the chair opposite Ethan's desk and braced his elbows on his knees. "You sure you know what you're doing?"

"No." Ethan rubbed his temples and shut his eyes. "But at this point I think I have to see it through."

"I get why Crabtree picked you to be his successor. You're just like the damn gangster, in love with the game."

Ethan opened his eyes and stared at the ceiling, hating the truth in Mitch's words. "I love Randy more than I love the game." Then he added, cautiously, "Do you think I should call it off?"

Mitch's grin sent a shiver down Ethan's spine. "Nah, not if you can win. Because like I said—that's why Randy picked you."

"He's always telling me not to play against Crabtree."

Mitch snorted. "Only because he knows you don't have the best of it. He's waiting for you to figure out how to get the better hand. Then you can play all you want."

"You don't think I have the best of it yet?"

"Don't know. Only you and he can sort that out. I sure as hell want you to beat that bastard's ass, so I'm all for it." He rose, tipping an imaginary hat to Ethan. "Go get 'em, Killer. My money's on you."

At first Ethan thought that was a metaphor, but then he realized where he was and winced. "There's a book on this? They're betting on what, exactly?"

"Fuck yeah. They're betting on who's going to smother the other one, you or Crabtree." Mitch said. "You're the only one not in yet. Want a piece?"

Ethan opened his mouth to say no, then paused. "The only one?"

Mitch winked. "Randy just put a grand on you."

"Wait. He bet on *me*? But this morning he acted like…" He frowned at the top of his desk, more confused than ever.

What in the world was going on here?

Ethan opened his laptop again with as much coolness as he could muster. "Mark me down for five thousand."

He managed to keep it together through Mitch's laugh and salute, not collapsing in cold fear onto his desk until the door had closed and he was alone again.

The casino Christmas party was beautiful, full of lights and music and laughter, but Randy had never felt less interested in the festivities around him.

He wanted to get this over with and get to the part where he was with Ethan and the others, the real Christmas he'd been dreaming of. This was supposed to be the best Christmas ever, and thanks to this fight between

Ethan and Crabtree it felt like it kept flirting with becoming the worst. Despite having Sam and Mitch present, they hadn't done anything Christmasy since these stupid Twelve Days of Randy had started. They'd fought, worried, and plotted. They hadn't gone to look at lights. They hadn't gone to any of the big casinos. They hadn't even been to the damn fountains. Randy felt so cheated. This should have been nothing but a Christmas orgasm, but it was nearly to the point that the sight of a Christmas tree had him tensing up.

Randy was tired of playing the clown for everyone at this party, and he was over this goddamn war between Ethan and Crabtree. Whatever novelty there had been to feeling like the princess in the tower had worn off long ago. This princess was about to get a fucking Uzi and order everybody to the floor.

Sam, unsurprisingly, had appointed himself honor guard, ramping up the charm when Randy couldn't muster it, generally deflecting what Randy wasn't up to managing. When he went to the bathroom to take a break and Sam followed, Randy pulled him into the shadows, drew him close, and kissed him hard in the center of his forehead.

Wrapping his arms around Randy's waist, Sam kissed his neck. "It'll be okay, Randy."

Randy shut his eyes, sucking in the smell of Sam's hair. "Goddamn it, but I love you, Peaches."

Sam's hand slid down to pinch his ass. "Come on. Splash some water on your face, and let's get back out there. It's almost time, and then this will be over. Mitch and I aren't going to get in line to save you some time. He says we're going to cut out early and go get ready for when you two can come home. He has the tamales all ready to go. Spicy pork and chicken."

Randy sighed, already imagining the taste. "Tamales. Now it really is Christmas with Mitch." He kissed Sam again. "And you too, baby."

"All of us," Sam agreed. "We're going to stay up late and have cocoa and cookies and watch movies with snow in them. And play Santa and the Naughty Elves."

"Yeah, and I'm going to spend an hour on Ethan's ass, the naughtiest elf of all." The visions Sam painted in Randy's head soothed and bolstered him. He drew a deep breath, stepped back, and squared his shoulders. "I don't need water. I'm ready. Bring it on, bitches."

On the casino floor, everyone had gathered around the fountain, where a large red and gold throne sat on a velvet-covered dais draped in enough evergreen branches to be its own ground-based tree. Randy suspected Caryle's work here, which stood to reason since her firm usually got hired for all the decorating at Herod's. Still, in his present mood it felt more than a little like *Et tu, Brute?*

He didn't let his irritation or his weariness show, though. He strode through the glittering Christmas wonderland, the great room dripping with multicolored lights and evergreen boughs, decked with red ribbons and golden tinsel. He smiled at the crowd of employees and guests clad in glitter and satin and velvet, everyone sipping drinks from fluted glasses, selecting tidbits from silver trays borne by handsome men and beautiful women.

Every last one of them can come up and

kiss me. Anywhere they want.

Why did this thought make Randy so annoyed? It was the sort of game he loved. Debauchery, free love—it meant nothing to him, not here, not tonight. It all felt hollow and empty, and not because this was also a pissing contest. That didn't help, but that wasn't what had his buns so toasted.

It was, he realized, that he finally had the Christmas he wanted within his reach, but he had to sit through this nonsense first, and he resented it. He knew this was important for Ethan so he could work Crabtree out of his system, but he was tired of being patient about it. He wished he would have taken Ethan up on his offer of cancelling this morning. If he had, they'd be at home now having a great time.

Except they wouldn't. Ethan would still have to be here as the owner. He'd still be chasing Crabtree.

Twelve damn days of giving himself away, and he was still waiting for the thing he wanted most.

Come on, Ethan. Give me a Christmas miracle.

Randy summoned an eager leer as they tied a red sash around his eyes. The crowd tittered and laughed as they lined up to have their turn for a kiss.

Ah, hell, this was going to be the longest night ever.

Randy's mask began to slip. Not literally—the damn blindfold was still in place, but his façade was no longer operational. He accepted kisses on his lips and his nose and on his cheek, and even one on his left knee, but when a drunken female staff member tried to pry apart his legs and kiss his belt buckle, he gently but firmly pushed her back and told her to give him one on his wrist and nothing else. The atmosphere mellowed after that, and Randy could tell as he received nothing but pecks on his temple from the next ten kissers that he'd put a damper on their fun.

Tough.

The crowd hushed again, and Randy tensed, because he knew what this meant. It was either Ethan or Crabtree coming up to him. This was pissing contest entry number one. Crabtree wouldn't kiss him anywhere near his face. He'd do something to get Randy shivering, then swoop in for the kill.

He could suck his own dick, because Randy wasn't shivering for anything, not tonight. If it was Ethan approaching him—well, Randy had put a grand on Ethan, so he wasn't going to deliberately shun his husband. Crabtree knew Randy had made the bet, so the gangster would try to rig this somehow. Goddamn this blindfold anyway—

He cut his internal rampage off as someone stopped at the foot of the dais. The casino went silent.

Randy dug his fingernails into the arms of the throne and shut his eyes against the red-tinged world of the blindfold, every cell in his body full of tension.

The dais shook under new weight as someone stepped in front of him. Then it shifted again.

Gentle fingers pried his right hand from the armrest, lifted it reverently as they turned Randy's hand over, and damp lips placed a soft, bone-melting kiss in the center of his palm.

Randy shivered.

When the man before him began to withdraw, Randy latched on to his hand. The gesture lifted him to his feet so he could stand, still blind, at the foot of his throne. There wasn't a single sound from their audience, and the man before him said nothing either. His thumb stroked the back of Randy's hand, though. Randy's heart, already willing to bet every stack he'd ever had that he knew who this was, rose through his chest to the top of his throat and pushed him all in.

Still blindfolded but no longer blind, Randy lifted his hands to the right height, grabbed his husband's face, and pulled him forward into a bruising kiss.

The crowd became a sea of whispers, but Randy didn't give a damn what they said. He just opened his mouth wider and swallowed more of Ethan, tasting his lips, his teeth, his tongue. His fingers shoved into the fragrant, familiar hair, cut so carefully, kept so tidy and clean. They strayed to the collar, crisp and ironed, to the suit coat, exquisitely tailored. They stole back up to his skin, soft and damp and vulnerable.

As his brain caught up with his body, he

stilled, startled, and then he laughed.

Ethan had won without trying, but now Randy understood why Ethan couldn't seem to believe him, what Crabtree had known and exploited simply because he was a slimy little bastard who liked to poke at people. Ethan couldn't *see* that he'd won.

Randy showed him.

After ripping off the blindfold, he opened his eyes just enough to steer Ethan around and slam him into the throne, at which point Randy climbed onto his lap and ground their hips together as he went in for another kiss. He held nothing back, only kissed him, over and over, his husband, his lover, his friend. He showed everyone how much he loved Ethan, let them see in the light how he kissed his husband in the dark. There was no debauchery, and Randy did not play the fool. He was the man who normally didn't let anyone see how much he wanted a sweet, old-fashioned Christmas full of sugar and spice and home and love.

For his final trick, Randy allowed the world to see that he was, in fact, a man who had that and more, with the man in his arms.

Eventually the terror of so much exposure caught up with him. Trembling, Randy stopped the kiss and sagged onto Ethan's shoulder.

The room broke out into applause. Randy lifted his head enough to scan the crowd, and he saw nothing but smiles and bright shining eyes. Also the back of Crabtree's head as he disappeared toward the elevator that would take him up to his office.

"That what you were hoping for, Slick?" he whispered into his neck.

Ethan gave a choked laugh and nuzzled his cheek. "Up until the last second, I'd meant to give you the kind of kiss you gave me. But when I saw how much this was getting to you, I realized this wasn't the way to do it at all."

Randy nipped at his chin. "I knew you by nothing more than the brush of your hand on mine. Which, if you recall, is exactly what I told you I could do."

"Even as angry as you were with me, you'll still kiss me like that?"

"I wasn't angry with you. I was frustrated because I want to get to the only celebration I care about, which is the one with you."

Ethan stroked Randy's cheek. "I finally figured it out, by the way, what you've been telling me about Crabtree and my need to win."

Randy raised an eyebrow. "Oh? Let's hear it."

"You kept saying you'd choose me over him, and I never doubted that, but it didn't seem like enough to me unless he saw you make that choice. When you knew me by only a simple touch, though, when I was trying to let you go and you pulled me in—that's when I realized. It wasn't ever Crabtree who needed to understand. It was me. My fear of my inadequacy was the problem all along. I was my own enemy. Why didn't you tell me I was playing poker with myself?"

"Because in my experience people have to fight their demons on their own. Though I admit I was about to come in and do some punching because I was tired of waiting. I should have known I wouldn't have to. You always come through in the end, baby." Randy ran a finger down Ethan's nose. "I don't want to kiss anyone else but you tonight. I don't care who that disappoints."

Ethan smiled and stroked his hip. "I think that's a wonderful idea. Why don't you go close up my office while I make our excuses and call up the car?"

Randy grinned. "Why don't I indeed?"

"Oh, but first—" Ethan withdrew a folded piece of paper from the inside of his jacket and handed it over. "Merry Christmas, Randy. A little early."

Randy opened the paper and frowned at it, not understanding. "Why am I looking at a photo of someone's house?"

"Because, if you take a tour of it and find it acceptable, it will eventually be *your* house." Ethan ran a finger under a series of smaller photos. "The kitchen is exceptional in this one, though there are a few other properties we've toured that you might want to consider as well."

Randy stared openmouthed, first at the paper, then at Ethan. "You…got me a…*house* for Christmas?"

"Well not *yet*. I'd never buy a house without your consent. I really can't tell about the kitchen. But Sam and Mitch helped, and—"

Ethan couldn't say anything else, not for

several minutes, because Randy's tongue was down his throat.

When Randy finally came up for air, he stroked his husband's face, nuzzling his nose. "You got me a house. With a fucking amazing kitchen. I love you. I cannot tell you how much I love you. Let me take you home and attempt to show you instead."

He started to rise, but Ethan pulled him back down. He took Randy's face gently in his hands and brushed a featherlight kiss against his lips. "Merry Christmas, Randy."

Merry Christmas to you too, Randy wanted to say, but his heart was overflowing. Christmas music played over the murmur of the crowd, fairy lights hung everywhere, and the air was full of the smell of rum and pine and Ethan. So he just smiled as he shut his eyes and leaned forward and kissed his husband.

Again.

Want to find out what happens next to the Special Delivery boys? The story continues in *Tough Love*, available now wherever books are sold.

It takes a strong man to be this fabulous.

Crescencio "Chenco" Ortiz pulled himself up by his garter straps after his father's will yanked the financial rug from under his spank-me pumps. He doesn't need anyone, yet when Steve Vance steps into his life, the prospect of having a sexy leather daddy on tap begins to take on a certain appeal.

There's a hitch when he learns Steve is friends with Mitch Tedsoe—the half-brother Chenco never knew except through his father's twisted lies. Despite his reservations, soon Chenco is living his dreams, including a performing gig in Vegas. Now if only he could get Steve to see him as more than just a boy in need of saving.

Steve's attraction to Chenco is overshadowed by too many demons, ones he knows his would-be lover is too young to slay. Yet as he gets to know the bright, determined young man whose drag act redefines *fierce,* Steve's inner sadist trembles with need. He begins to realize Chenco's relentless tough love might be the only thing that will finally set him free.

ABOUT THE AUTHOR

Heidi Cullinan has always enjoyed a good love story, provided it has a happy ending. Proud to be from the first Midwestern state with full marriage equality, Heidi is a vocal advocate for LGBT rights. She writes positive-outcome romances for LGBT characters struggling against insurmountable odds because she believes there's no such thing as too much happy ever after. When Heidi isn't writing, she enjoys cooking, reading, playing with her cats, and watching anime, with or without her family. Find out more about Heidi at heidicullinan.com.

Did you enjoy this book?

If you did, please consider leaving a review online or recommending it to a friend. There's absolutely nothing that helps an author more than a reader's enthusiasm. Your word of mouth is greatly appreciated and helps me sell more books, which helps me write more books.

OTHER TITLES IN THIS SERIES

SPECIAL DELIVERY

Sam knows he'll never find the excitement he craves in Middleton, Iowa. Then Sam meets Mitch, an independent, long-haul trucker. When Mitch offers to take him on a road trip west, Sam jumps at the chance. One minute Mitch is the star of Sam's X-rated fantasies, the next he's a perfect gentleman. And when they hit the Las Vegas city limit, Sam finds out why: Randy. Sam grapples with the meaning of friendship, letting go, growing up—even the meaning of love—because no matter how far he travels, eventually all roads lead home.

HOOCH AND CAKE

All Sam and Mitch want to do is get married, but between their busy schedules and the judgment of a small town, it's not as easy as it should be. Then their best friend Randy shows up, and the wedding that almost wasn't is about to become the wedding Iowa never dreamed to see.

DOUBLE BLIND

Randy can't stand to just sit by and watch as a mysterious man throws money away on roulette. The man's dark desperation has him scrambling for a reason—any reason—to save his soul. Ethan has no idea what he's going to do with himself once his last dollar is gone—until Randy whirls into his life with a heart-stealing smile and a poker player's gaze that sees too much. Soon they're both taking risks that not only play fast and loose with the law, but with the biggest prize of all: their hearts.

TOUGH LOVE

Chenco Ortiz harbors fierce dreams of being a drag star on a glittering stage, but when leatherman Steve Vance introduces him to the intoxicating world of sadomasochism, he finds strength in body and mind he's never dreamed to seek—strength enough maybe to save his tortured Papi too.

OTHER BOOKS BY HEIDI CULLINAN

There's a lot happening with my books right now! Sign up for my **release-announcement-only newsletter** on my website to be sure you don't miss a single release or rerelease.

www.heidicullinan.com/newssignup

Want the inside scoop on upcoming releases, automatic delivery of all my titles in your preferred format, with option for signed paperbacks shipped worldwide? Consider joining my Patreon.

www.patreon.com/heidicullinan

THE ROOSEVELT SERIES
Carry the Ocean (also available in French)
Shelter the Sea
Unleash the Earth (coming soon)
Shatter the Sky (coming soon)

LOVE LESSONS SERIES
Love Lessons (also available in German; French coming soon)
Frozen Heart
Fever Pitch (also available in German)

Lonely Hearts (also available in German)
Short Stay
Rebel Heart (coming soon)

THE DANCING SERIES
Dance With Me (also available in French; Italian coming soon)
Enjoy the Dance
Burn the Floor (coming soon)

MINNESOTA CHRISTMAS SERIES
Let It Snow
Sleigh Ride
Winter Wonderland
Santa Baby

CHRISTMAS TOWN SERIES
The Christmas Fling

THE SPECIAL DELIVERY SERIES
Special Delivery
Hooch and Cake
Double Blind
The Twelve Days of Randy
Tough Love

CLOCKWORK LOVE SERIES
Clockwork Heart
Clockwork Pirate (coming soon)
Clockwork Princess (coming soon)

TUCKER SPRINGS SERIES
Second Hand (written with Marie Sexton)
(available in French)
Dirty Laundry (available in French)
(more titles in this series by other authors)

SINGLE TITLES
Nowhere Ranch (available in Italian)
Family Man (written with Marie Sexton)
A Private Gentleman
The Devil Will Do
Hero
Miles and the Magic Flute

NONFICTION
Your A Game: Winning Promo for Genre Fiction (written with Damon Suede)

Many titles are also available in audio and more are in production. Check the listings wherever you purchase audiobooks to see which titles are available.

CPSIA information can be obtained
at www.ICGtesting.com
Printed in the USA
LVHW090241040821
694506LV00012B/172

9 781945 116254